A PRODIGAL BASTARD

VOLUME I

The

ESCAPE FROM MICTLÁN

Trilogy

WILL LORIMER

ISBN 978-1-8381382-0-2

INKISTAN
.COM

In 1936, André Breton declared that Mexico was the most surreal country in the world.

Salvador Dali never went to Mexico because he believed he could never go to a country that was more surreal than himself.

PRÓLOGO

Rain was falling in sheets, the college campus dark and deserted. The hazy outlines of its postmodern buildings could have been the towers of a long-abandoned city, lost in gloom but for a haloed light spearing from the farthest block.

Behind the steamed-up glass of that one unboarded ground-floor window, two men, obviously arguing. The nearest, broader in the beam than he stood. Yea, not to put too fine a point on it, borderline midget, back turned, fists bunched at his sides. His mustard jacket and flaming red hair, fluorescent in the harsh neon light. The other, by his white shirt, black tie and rigid demeanour, clearly an official, sat behind a desk, empty but for a phone.

Though unseen in the darkness, my arrival outside the window had heralded an impasse of sorts, but then the official seemed to relent, reached into a drawer of his desk and, after a pause, passed something thin over. The stocky wee man hastily pocketed whatever it was and turned around, presenting a face I had never seen before.

But at least I had his name right. It seemed to fit his angry glare as he stepped out into the rain, and, though he did not have a droopy moustache to match his red hair, to me he was still the mad Mexican of the *Loony Tunes* cartoons I so loved as a child.

As I introduced myself, Wee Donald's beady eyes glinted, he flashed a broken-toothed grin then punched me hard in the ribs.

As I rubbed my side, he growled in a thick accent of the old country, 'Ach, I remember ye now! Y'er a fuckin' prayer answered, just when I need ye's. Yesterday my brother was swept away in a flood in fuckin' Can-ad-a!'

He spat each syllable. 'Can-ad-a!' D'ye ken whit tha' means? It's Spanish, *ca nada*, eh! Meaning there's nothin' there. The wurds o' a Spanish sailor, looking oot tae the fogbanks o' Labrador, frae the furst galleon passin'. *Ca nada*,' he repeated, in a climaxing dirge.

'Well noo,' he sighed. 'That's true. An' today I learned,' he grinned, a characteristic of hard men of the old country imparting bad news, 'I wuz sacked six months ago from this dump.' He gave me a new look of approbation, implying I'd earned at least a quantum of respect. 'You're fuckin' lucky tae catch me, I wuz only here tae collect the outstanding.' He brandished a thin envelope. 'This, my wife says, is all that's stonding between wir family an' destitution.' His jaw jutted. 'But I say it's beer money,' he said, extending broad hands, 'And you're my first foot from hame in mair than twen'y years.' He wiped a tear from an eye as he embraced me. 'I love you brother,' he sobbed, resting his red head against my chest as I wondered how the fuck I had gotten there.

In the small hours of the day the lease on my Greenwich Village apartment was up. I was awoken by the phone ringing off the hook, and with a name tipping my tongue. Yea, I knew that caller hanging on the line. Ignoring her insistent clamour, I thumbed the dog-eared pages of my address book, until my index finger stopped on the name of a professor of Meso-American studies, under a college address in Mexico City. I couldn't fix the face, but as I closed the apartment door, leaving the phone to ring on, I recalled our chance meeting on an ancient mound in the middle of desolate moor, Macbeth country.

On the summit loomed three standing stones known as the 'little sisters', huddled over the 'cauldron', a truncated black stone cupping the sky in a pool of rainwater. Mist coiled, the clouds were low and the wind biting. I was there with a party of friends, but had drifted away, when we struck up conversation, while watching a small police car approaching slowly along a long straight track, from where the distant hills blurred into the sky, making the moorland seem a desolation that went on forever. We heard the car stop out of sight below, before two red-faced policemen clambered panting over the brow of the mound. Yes, even in that remoteness, there was no escape from the long arm of the law. I'd heard the news item on the radio that morning, and now two police constables were delivering it to a friend in my party. It seemed that the elderly couple who drove their BMW into a dry dock in Blackpool had been his parents. I didn't know whether to be glad or sad they weren't mine, but I did get that college address.

Despite or because of all the threats and insults, the driver of the taxi I'd hired at the airport, depleting what remained from my cards, emptied at the ATMs of la Guardia, refused to drive to Wee Donald's locale, and instead set us down in pouring rain at a deserted street corner, some distance away.

'Pussy,' Wee Donald called after the departing cab, its one tail light blurring in the rain before it disappeared, a red streak into a maze of darkened back streets.

'What's the problem?' I asked, looking down at my bags and the crate of beer Wee Donald had just bought at a 24-hour *cerveceria*.

'Och,' Wee Donald shrugged, 'A few mair murders and kidnappings than usual these past months.'

'Really?' I said, more alarmed by his nonchalance than anything.

'Ach dae fuss ye'rself.' He grinned, 'Ye're wi' me. Everything's perrrfectly safe! I'll show ye's.' Wee Donald cupped his hands about his mouth. 'Fuck yuz cunts!' he bellowed at the shuttered windows of tenements on all sides. 'Come and get uz, assholes.'

'That just proves you're mental,' I laughed, as his challenge boomed back, echoing empty city streets.

'Aye,' Wee Donald nodded, 'But mental means too much fuckin' bother tae the gangs roond here. Besides,' he grinned, 'They're a' boys, no real men like uz. C'mon,' he said, heaving the beer crate onto a broad shoulder, 'We've a wake tae get oan wi'.'

The block where Wee Donald lived appeared archaic and semi-derelict, sandwiched as it was between a sports arena with giant posters of masked wrestlers by its closed doors and the glass building of a TV corporation, with giant satellite dishes on its roof. At street level was a line of small shops, all shuttered, while the windows of the floors above, were oddly juxtaposed, and of different sizes and styles, suggesting the old building had been rebuilt, more than once.

'Bonny, eh?' Wee Donald said, nodding towards a woman, who briefly appeared, looking out of an upper floor window, her face underlit, red and green by a fizzing neon sign, which featured a cherry and a lime in a cocktail glass, blinking red and green, at the corner of the block.

'If you say so,' I shrugged, wondering if the woman was his wife.

'No' her,' Wee Donald grinned, '*Her.*' he waved his free hand, taking in the whole building. 'Look at thae lines mon. Dae they no' remind ye o' a ship o' state, magnificent eh? Originally that was whaur Prince Falling Eagle hung out. Yes, it was Cuhuatomec's fuckin' palace. The last Aztec building left standing in Mexico shitty,' he laughed, with a sweep of his hand including the whole city, 'Though o' course it's much broken doon noo. Dates back tae 'afore the Conquest.' He pointed to the lower facade. 'See where that plaster's fallen awa', yon stane's the pink o' auld Tenochtitlán.'

'Pay any nae heed tae the wife,' Wee Donald cautioned over a heavy Latin beat from somewhere below, leading the way up worn wooden steps. 'She cannae abide me drinkin,' he chortled, 'But that's her fuckin' problem, no' mine.' Throwing open the front door, he waved me in.

In a small dingy kitchen, Wee Donald's wife was on her knees, polishing pairs of kiddies' shoes. By the tears stains on her sallow cheeks and her bleary red eyes, she had been weeping a week. Hung on the back of a chair were school uniforms, a girl's and a boy's, neatly pressed.

'Oh god, not more beer,' she bleated, her accent redolent of Pimms, cucumber sandwiches and croquet on green summer lawns. Flicking a couple of strands of lank brown hair from her eyes she noticed me over the crate on Wee Donald's broad shoulder. 'And who's this?' her thin lips twisted. 'Another stray from the street?'

'A freend a' the way frae the auld country, so you be mindin' yer manners, hen,' Wee Donald glowered.

'Welcome, I'm sure,' the English wife muttered, resuming polishing shoes, which, in the dingy kitchen, shone with a brilliance that was almost supernatural. 'Your other *friends* are

11

in the back,' she added, as under her knees the floorboards began to shake, and the Latin music below increased in volume. 'How do you put up with that racket? I said, following Wee Donald's dancing zigzag course, hefting his beer crate with surprising agility to avoid the various tins that had been strategically positioned to catch the steady dripping of water from gaping holes in the plaster ceiling.

Twisting around, he raised a finger to his mouth. 'Ssh,' he cautioned, swaying uncertainly, 'Dinnae want tae wake them.' He pointed through the glass door of a bedroom where two children lay sleeping. Just their small faces above bunched covers, blinking pink, white, green, and back again, as the neon sign below their window fizzed and sparked in the heavy rain. 'Aye, I ken what ye'r thinking, son.' Wee Donald grinned fiendishly in the lurid light. 'Yon's Mexico's national colours! C'mon.' He turned, resuming his balancing act, like a footballer jinxing the opposition, dodging tackles – only they were tins – on into the gloom of the dingy passage, throbbing with the sound of Santana from below.

'That's our resident DJ doon stairs in the ... heh ... heh trannie brothel,' he called back.

'A transvestite brothel? You're putting me on,' I laughed.

'See for yerself,' Wee Donald said, stopping, his florid face under-lit by a roseate glow as, swaying, he pointed to a crack in the bare boards by his feet. Enough of a gap to make out a giant pink puffball and the bouffant hairstyle of an Elvis wannabe in a sequin suit on a stage directly below.

'That's the tosser at his decks,' Wee Donald sniggered. 'Thinks he's the king o' fuckin' Graceland. I only wish he'd play something apart frae fuckin' "Black Magic Wumman".'

At the end of the passage a door opened into a lounge

furnished in contemporary, if conventional, style, hung with framed lithographs of Mayan temples. It was uninhabitable, however, since a large section of the ceiling had fallen onto the sofa and carpet with the start of the seasonal rains a few days before.

Behind another door, six bearded anthropologists in worsted jackets were crammed into a narrow, smoke-filled study, done up like a train carriage, its walls decorated with railway memorabilia from the old country, and black and white photographs of Wee Donald's school days. The general familiarity of the images, together with the rusting enamel signs from the Age of Steam, made me feel I was trapped in a time tunnel as I sat on the edge of a chaise longue beside two Mexican men - obviously *caballeros*, since both wore posh tweed jackets -- swapping insults and turns as they played backgammon for high stakes that, with every few rolls of the dice, kept doubling. A stack of US dollars beside the board on the table staked against a set of keys for a Cherokee 4x4 and a kilo bag of smelly grass buds.

It was a fine wake and, as the night wore on, talk turned to a recent find by one of the group in a Mayan pyramid threatened by a new highway being cut through the jungle in Quintana Roo. If the artefacts in the unopened chamber weren't removed soon, the precious hoard would be looted by the *jefé* of the road gang. A rescue mission was proposed, and I was invited to join what could be a rewarding adventure.

But I had other plans in mind, and so, my head swimming from booze and dope, I left the claustrophobic study and wearily climbed some steep wooden stairs to a flat roof, hemmed in by the giant satellite dishes of a TV relay station on one side and the curving roof of the sports arena on the other.

13

It was when I saw the blue flashes of electric plasma, rimming the big satellite dishes and striking upwards in a column of rising sparks from the dome of the sports arena, that my head exploded. Through slashing rain, outlined in a luminous interplay of banded colours, soaring out of a purple backdrop of cumulus cloud, the shadow play of the three puppeteers of my existence. Gods or demons, I didn't know, though the thought did intrude that my life was hanging in the balance; in an abyssal realm higher powers were dickering, my fate being decided, as I stood transfixed.

I

El SOL DE LA MUERTE ...

Looking out of a dusty bus window, I was half blinded by an engorged red eye, spiked on three black peaks rearing the high chapparal. Silhouetted sierras, pointy witches hats in huddle, casting inky shadows across a scratchy expanse of tarbrush back-lit like the set of Mexican snuff flick. And the sun? Going down to do battle with the astral armies of the night. To return? Once that depended on the valour of the vanquished, who if the chroniclers of the Spanish Conquest were to be believed, were sacrificed in their thousands on Aztec pyramids, drenched in blood. A crimson tide that by the evidence of my eyes, still lapped the desert hereabouts.

'*Mira! El sol de la muerte!*' Interrupting my mental drift, the hirsute smoker from the seat behind, blowing smoke in my ear, leaning on my shoulder, jabbing his *cigarro* at an angry face glaring in a bus window.

'The sun of death,' I recycled, turning away from the roadside telegraph poles, strobing past my grimy window. Do

17

re mi, the wires carrying messages I didn't want to hear. This joker with the shaggy black dog moustache, breathing brimstone and beer in my ear, giving the local weather lore. Wanting me to believe that the sombrero corona brimming the sun indicated bad weather on the road ahead. Considering the high cirrus clouds, I supposed he was probably right. But then the advancing weather front, might just as well have been tendrils of racked seaweed, seen from the deck of the ship of my drowned hopes, spiralling down to Davey Jones' locker room, in the depths of the Sargasso Sea.

'*Muy mallow para el gringo!*' he insisted in guttural Spanish even worse than mine, suggesting that Nahuatl, the ancient language of these remote parts, was his mother tongue.

But when I shrugged, wondering what was so bad for this *gringo* in particular, he seemed to take the hump and sat back down with a bump, raising a squawk from his prize cockerel in a crate on the wooden seat beside him. Bemused, I turned away and finally got the picture. Glaring through the bus window, not the sun king in a sombrero, his valour guard trailing sparks over the *sierras*, but the grinning skull of a ghostly bandit chief – Pancho Villa, or some such masked desperado, holed up since *la Revoluçion*. Every night, come hail, thunder and lightning, going down on the three sisters, riding out on the broomstick of the tarbrush horizon, flying over bandit badlands, spiked as a flagellant's cloak.

Mexico, more than a pilgrimage, *mucho mas*.

And now, cupped by a black caldera, pinioned by three purple-robed eminences, a shimmering egg, shrinking into a snake of gold descending between vitrine peaks, cracking the world. Captured in an eidetic blink a burning nest high in a tree, hatching a baby snake that changed into a yellow oriole bird and flew away chirping into the blue.

Was that an image from the never-neverland land of lost childhood or a long-forgotten dream? How could I ever know; my memory was so porous. And no, it wasn't just the drugs. If I survived the next leg, there would be time for the exercises my analyst had prescribed for memory retrieval, supposed, turning to look out the window again, as a fleeting shadow crossed over and I caught a glimpse of wing tips as an unnaturally large black bird swept low above.

Another sign as the little bus banded red and green, the colours of *Líneas Fronteras*, the only bus company serving these remote parts, lurched from uncertain asphalt to more certain cobbles, paused, gathering energy before the assault on bandit foothills. There, at the turn, a crude sign with the words '*Trópico de Cancer*' grooved on bleached wood, marking the crossing of a boundary..

Behind me now routes *norté* and the junk of my past. Was that phone still ringing, in my old apartment? I could still hear it. No matter, what glittered was baubles and trinkets. Slow lanes on a fast track, jumping saddle to saddle. Haymaking in the fields of my youth which once was sheaved with golden stacks blowing chaff in the wind, but now, entering my thirties, all I had was a fistful of corn slipping my grasp.

I was here, too, sheltering in a geological book so vast I couldn't make out the pages. There, high on the haunch of some antediluvian beast, my name in big letters on copper banded scree, proving I had made it – if not hereafter, then *sic gloria transit*, as a bishop might have opined. Quinton, after my paternal grandfather; Eric, from a Laplander great-uncle on my mother's side, no doubt a tall straw-haired numbskull like myself; Diogenes, from when I slept in a bathtub in a flat shared by three girls who took pity on my homeless condition and nicknamed me after the cynic philosopher. I loved them so much I adopted the moniker by deed poll, and signed QED with a flourish on a bouncing cheque at the restaurant where we dined, after I flunked out of university without a degree, but with sad parting kisses from all three, who might have been sisters they were so similar in looks, though not nature. In the plain words of a dead language, *quo erat demonstrandum*, meaning thus proved the proposition. An absent father's pronouncement, I imagined, upon receiving the news of my latest failure from Mr Crook. Not that the well-worn Latin phrase would have meant anything to the other passengers – all *mestizos*, Native American genes predominating. All moustachioed, *machos* and *muchachas*, bumping two and three to a seat, like this was the love bus to Cancun, hanging on, hanging in, even the goggle-eyed turkey, dangling over the back of a portacabin squaw blocking the aisle of the bus, joining in the fun. I was alone, a stranger in the midst of one big happy family.

We had reached a way station in a gloomy gully, the most level gradient thus far. Even so, all that prevented the little bus from rolling back the way we had come was a rock wedged in under the nearside front tyre, parked perilously close to the sagging roofs of some shacks shedding tiles, just below – telescoping terracotta dammed by the roadside ridge. A whole tribe lived down there. At the head of a steep path, by the open bus door, three, four generations. Gaunt, pubescents; tots saddled on hips. More barefoot children clutching the torn skirts of bent-backed crones, who might yet be in only their thirties, I guessed, watching them passing back plastic containers filled with water, careful not to spill a precious drop. Out front, *el commandanté* bus driver doing much the same. Just the shiny brim of his cap and gold star, lost in a rush of steam as he refilled the radiator. Ahead, cresting the long spine of the canyon, a pair of lofty pines, black against the electric *sierra* twilight, marking a gateway, a couple of stars pirouetting in the azule – astral outriders from the netherworld.

I was jolted back to the *now* by a young girl standing outside at the bus window, staring out of my mirror image on darkening glass. Under the brim of my black hat, which we both shared in the window, my pale foreign face, her Toltec eyes, my Castilian chin, her chapped cheeks, my mercenary jowl, her tribe's pain, absolved in a new world trigonometry, proving that victim and oppressor can be the same. Of course I was a *gringo*, with my green eyes and pale skin, no one could mistake me for anything else.

But she was safe with me, and could keep her virtue intact, the only treasure she had left. No, not I. Not a drop of bastard conquistador blood in my veins. Well, none that I knew of.

'... neh ... neh ... neh ...' that was the nasal sniggering, issuing the barrel-chested *hombre* sitting next to me, snoring since Chihuahua with his sombrero over his face. Now its brim was pushed back on sharp black eyes focused on the Super Lights in my denim breast pocket – Yankee cigarettes, another form of currency in out-of-the-way places south of the Rio Grandé. Good for petty bribes and breaking the ice.

'... neh ... neh ... neh ...' he continued irritatingly as I split the soft pack and, with a practiced slap to the base, raised a couple of butts to order. Slyly, he took one, tucked that behind an ear, winked and reached out again.

'Go on,' I said, 'They're only *dirty* frees.' Of course I meant to say 'duty'. Same difference, sometimes.

'... neh-neh-neh ... *gracías señor*,' he managed between nasal snickers, grinning hugely, revealing a mouth full of gum boils pegged down by a few decayed stumps, like the remnants of an old sea pier washed by black tides.

'*De nada*,' I shrugged, flicking a flame on my old brass zippo, thinking of neurotics I had known who would have simply expired at such a sight. Yet he seemed hale and hearty. Perhaps those pustules actually kept him healthy.

After cogitating on nicotine, recycling smoke via stained

moustaches and flaring nostrils – an economy measure born of hard times? – a grimy finger prodded in my direction again ...

'Ahem ...' he coughed unconvincingly. Perhaps he thought this to be the correct way to initiate a conversation with a *caballero* – I *was* dressed in the best of British worsted gear; in Mexico, apparently, such apparel denoted a gentleman of worth. '*Tiene niños, señor?*'

'*Si* ...' I replied, as termite eyes bored in.

'*Hijos o hijas?*' He was asking if I had sons or daughters.

Thinking of that Toltec girl last seen through a bus window, '*Niñas*,' I sighed. '*Ey tu?*'

'*Hijos!*' he snapped, raising a fist – a hard-on for the universe, the bus and me.

'*Cuantas niñas tiene, señor?*' He grinned, eyes like he was hypnotising a snake. That snake was me. Perhaps he was after my cigarettes or wallet, or both? The Third World over, card-carrying *gringos* are excluded from age-old laws of hospitality. I guessed, given half a chance, those mountain natives would rob you of all you owned, but – since they *were* mountain natives – if they found you hungry and alone, they would snatch the tortillas from the mouths of their *bambinos* to feed you. Probably put you up in the only bed, if they had one ...

Randomly, I held up two fingers, by way of an answer. Perhaps it was the *mezcal?* I wondered, the glittering of his dark eyes reminding me of distant flares – the Pémex refinery passed in the desert – just gas burning off; in his case, I supposed cactus spirits. Probably home-brewed *mezcal* from the agave plants dotting the mountain side. I wondered if he was carrying any. Sure would relieve the tedium.

A question seemed expected. After all, we were discussing

the relative merits of our respective, in my case fictional, families, even if we were both doing so in broken Spanish, which for him, being a native of these mountains, I supposed was a second language.

'Y *tu?*' I asked him.

'*Diez!*' again *el borracho* shot up a fist, first fanning and then retracting his fingers, in the manner of bookmakers at racecourses, mental defectives and dealers in futures markets.

'Ten! And *hijos* too!' I exclaimed, entering the number in my notebook, for his benefit, 'You old *macho* son of a gun, you.' I winked, knowing in such conversations language is not a barrier. It was obvious, the sperm count rose with elevation. Clearly, it was the altitude that counted, not the attitude. We were still climbing. The desert plains, now miles below, those Pémex flares still burning, way off in the west. A world away on this cobbled old road winding three sisters towards a glittering Horus eye, the shining capstone of an icy peak reflecting the last rays of the sun, heading towards a tunnel leading to the other side of this untoward Mexican reality.

Another question seemed imminent as, with a lurch of the bus, he shouldered in, boss-eyed with determination to get whatever it was off his barrel chest.

'*Cigarillos?*' I ventured, wondering how I was supposed to reach my breast pocket when we were chin to chin.

'*Qué pasa?*' I said into his blind stare.

'*Señor,*' he smiled, '*Tiene los mismos ojos que la bruja de la norté.*'

'You're saying I have eyes the same as the *bruja* of the north?' I recycled, hoarsely.

'*Si,*' he nodded. Clearly satisfied he'd sussed me out, he

settled back against his seat. More than I had at that moment, I reflected. But the last detail suggested I was on the right track, and that somewhere up in the mountains were the answers I needed to penetrate the shifting fogs of an amnesia my New York analyst, a practitioner of the Now School of Therapy, failed to dispel, concealing an early childhood trauma, lurking just out of mind in reoccurring nightmares ever since, reaching across the years like the left hand of darkness.

2

EL TÚNEL

We had reached Capstone Canyon. Sheer ice walls ascending to Asgard via haberdasheries and a black void. Dead ahead, the way through to Valhalla, where Woden and Votan were waiting. Mixing my mythic metaphors again, but then in the Nordic and Central American legends both were travelling tricksters who 'measured the world' and wore black hats with big brims and matching cloaks: a dress code that Cortez adopted on the advice of the witch Malinché, who had him delay landfall in the Americas to coincide with the prophesied day of Votan's return. Like myself, I reflected, cloaked in darkness, hiding my pale face below a black brim. Ahead, the gaping tunnel; at first glance, less an entrance and more a mouth, stalactites of ice spectral in the beam of a lone headlight, so many fangs of a canine bite. Cerberus perhaps, or just the hound of the Baskervilles – different cultures, same myth. Closer, a rustic cabin set-down on the icy ground as if it had been helicoptered up from the Tyrol. The shingle roof dusted by snow, wide eaves sheltering a billy goat, bearded as Satan at a sabbat, yellow eyes luminescent in the glare of our bus' headlight, tethered to wooden boards banded familiar red and green, suggesting a far-flung outpost of empire. A supposition confirmed when, straight out of an old comic book, goose-stepped a major-domo buttoned up to his chin in the livery of *Líneas Fronteras*. A hat to cap our bus driver's;

bigger, grander, more gold braiding. Seven-pointed stars like on the Australian flag, suggesting that the story of the Ozzie explosives experts, employed in the mines hereabouts, might be true. An impressive sight, certainly, as he marched across the frozen ground to the driver's window and tore a ticket out of a little book, receiving a dirty ten peso note in exchange, then saluting smartly, stepping back, and we were moving once more, heading for an icy black hole.

Mary, Mother of God. Jesus, blessed redeemer, protect us from *gnomos malvados* that dwell under the earth ... well, something like that. Then, more gabbled prayers from the passengers, as we entered a rough-hewn passage, its walls riddled with voids that I supposed were old mines. But that wasn't all. After about five minutes, the little bus stopped at a branching of the passageway, prompting another mad session of furtive crossing and native mumbo-jumbo. Not because of our driver's uncertainty over directions, as I had assumed, but a candlelit grotto to the right side. Bus exhausts fanning an avenue of wavering flames, leading to an altar cleaved out of living rock, below a gnarled white Christ impaled on stellate pickaxes and shovels, the polished metal of the implements gleaming in the gloom.

'Neh neh neh,' a familiar nasal snicker sounded in my right lug hole. '*Es una MADERA!*'

'Yea, yea, I can see that,' I smiled, glad to see my companion back to his *borracho* best. 'It's made out of wood.'

'*No, no, señor.*' Pointing with a stubby finger, he leaned heavily across me. '*Ese Cristo nació en la madera.*'

'Born in the wood,' I repeated, peering through dirty window glass. 'Yes, I can see now the statue's naturally formed,' I said, noticing the pale bark was stippled like that of white oak. 'How odd.'

'*Es un milagroso*,' he insisted slyly.

'Sure,' I smiled, reminded of the frequency of miracles in Mexico, wondering how much more ubiquitous, then, in the last unmapped range in Central America. Unmapped? Because, as Wee Donald went on to explain, invariably the three sisters were blanketed in cloud, while magnetic anomalies and the frequent storms made aerial reconnaissance simply too dangerous.

'*De hace mucho tiempo.*'

'From the old days, uh-huh,' I nodded.

'*Cuando las tres hermanitas estaban cubiertas del Arboles.*' He went on, confirming at least I'd guessed right the local name of the mountains.

'When trees covered the three little sisters?' I exclaimed, forgetting in my excitement a pair of lofty pines, last seen from the bus stop, silhouetted on the *sierra* skyline. 'I don't believe you.'

'*Si, señor, antes de los conquistadores, las sierras eran un jardin mas sagrado.*'

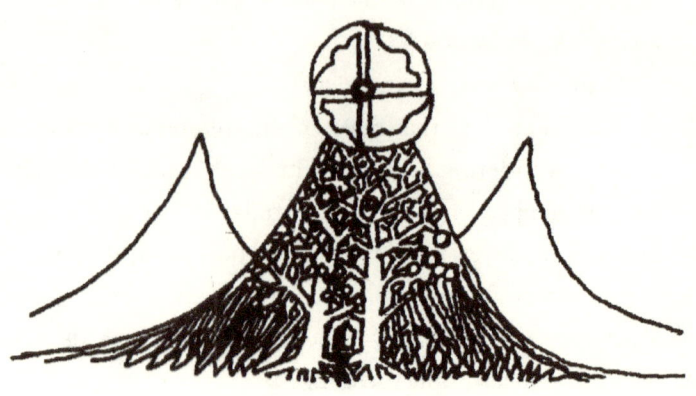

'A sacred garden, my god, yes, I can see that.' I muttered, in my mind the lost pieces of a jigsaw reforming, as I pictured the fabled garden, which in the legends was guarded by the three daughters of *night*. 'Then, after the Conquest,' I continued excitedly, 'All the trees were cut-down for pit props. Yea, all the locals converted at the point of a sword, and indentured in the new mines. Their only solace, Jesus, the living spirit of the garden, pointing the way through to the ...'

Fortunately, before I could turn even more pedantic, movement, blessed movement. Up front, our steersman, outlined against the moving picture projected on a windscreen by the bus' wayward eye. The one headlight illuminating incoming ... rough-cut, choppy waves, the tunnel walls flashing silver as if shoals of swordtails were passing through. Once a phantom party shouldering picks and shovels, shielding their eyes as we shaved past. Miners I supposed, heading to the Chapel of the Lost Christ, to kneel before starting the back shift, in one of the many shafts leading off the tunnel.

3

IN TOWN, LOOKING
ABOUT...

Last off and last in, everyone else scattered to the four corners, not even echoing footsteps to guide me, stumbling over the rutted cobbles that served for a street; a Mexican stand-off of slab-sided buildings, outlined in a lightning flash, vaulted stone aspiring to crow steps and turrets. Did I say Mexico? More like a stage set for Don Giovanni. Bring on the kettle drums. Now the lightning forking on fifteenth-century Pamplona, minus the frills. A medieval slum town after the plague, following the footsteps of the Grim Reaper. All the population, with the exception of the town doctor and a black cat, in mass graves or long since rotted behind boarded doors. Wee Donald had been right. This ghost town was the best preserved, most authentic and least-known *pueblo fantasmos fabulosa* in all of the Americas, the Town With No Name. Surpassing strange, yet eerily familiar, as if I had been here before. An impossibility, but then so was this medieval town and those three sisters above, their jagged peaks, vivid in a lightning strike. As if all were coexisting in a Möbius present, that would have been doubly perfect, had not I recalled my secret purpose, born out of a past that was nothing if not imperfect – and questions, so many questions, about missing chapters in my palimpsest, scattered life.

One more thing to do, but first I had overcome this overwhelming desire to turn and run, all the way back to my old brownstone apartment. Shutting my eyes, I could almost hear that phone still ringing as I raced up the stairs and flung open the door. But, I reminded myself, that was then and this was now. And, as my analyst might have said, the eternal NOW is always moving on.

The past? *No existé nada*; only the present. Who knows what might transpire? I must forget my dragon Chinese landlady and lately hard-to-please lover, and our metro-life that never was in her refurbed duplex on 5th Avenue. My analyst was right, this was something I had to face on my own.

I opened my eyes. The ringing stopped. Before me was a heavy looking door, its blackened stone lintel, carved with sheaves of corn and the Roman numerals MCDXXXII – if my prep-school Latin served me correctly – dating the building to sixty years *before* Columbus landed in the Americas, just as I had been assured. And, above that, a rusting sign painted with the  faded legend, '*La Castilla del Dinero*', swaying slightly in the gusting wind. Its slow creaking, I realised, translating in my head, as the ringing of a phone. There was nothing else to do, but take courage in both my hands, along with that door knocker.

Just audible, shuffling steps, then high on the door a small panel sliding back on a metal grill and, behind that, a suspicious eye, green as the ice on Scapa Flow, ringed with mascara. I knew that eye, no mistaking its baleful glare.

'We are closed for the season. Go *away!* '

'Nope,' I folded my arms, 'I'm staying put till you open that

34

door ... *Helga.'*

'How you know my name? Who are you?'

'Don't you recognise me?' I grinned, pushing my face up to the grill. 'I've only come halfway across the bleeding world to find you.'

'What you want? It is much too late in the night for silly games.'

'Let me in!' I kicked the door, a familiar blood rage taking hold. 'You won't shut me out this time ... *Mummy.'*

That was the magic password –the open sesame even *she* could not refuse. Yes, she was my mother. So long absent but never forgotten. How could I? What memories I retained were so traumatic – wherever *she* was thunder and lightning were always close. Folded in my wallet an old magazine cutting, snapped arm in arm with my father, their faces lit up by flashbulbs, entering a London society fancy dress ball – a pouting Amazon, stacked in matching silver stetson and stilettos, looming over a Roman proconsul in toga and circlet of laurel. Unchanged as far as I could gather, except she was now clad in a plaid dressing gown instead of burlesque Scythian chariot gear. Still, looking down, after all these years, in her right hand a candle, in her left anodised metal. A pistol, small but deadly, no doubt. Palmed into a pocket as she pulled open the heavy creaking door. Yes, the same hand that rocked my cradle. There are mothers and there are *mothers*. Mine was a crocodile from before the flood, and the mud-banks of a primordial swamp; such was my fate. Was that karma, over from a previous life? If so my crimes must have been prodigal. But whatever the truth of that, I deserved her, because fool that I was I'd actually searched her out. Now *that* I couldn't believe.

Mummy ...

(*an inside view*)

4

LA BRUJA DEL NORTÉ

Soon as I put a foot over the threshold, like I'd tripped a switch, the lobby light flashed on. Then, as the heavy door slammed shut behind me, a more distant clap of thunder announced the storm was passing.

'My *gott* Quinton!' Helga smiled, pinching the candle flame, clearly far more amazed by the light coming on, than by my sudden reappearance after such a considerable time. 'You bring luck to the house. The first time the electricity is on for a week.' She frowned. 'Look at that,' she tutted at hot wax dripping gloss red talons, held up to the light. 'How I hates the *borrachos* down at the *éstacion*, always drunk out their *pocito* skulls.'

'That bad, is it?' I said, glad of small talk and distraction from the assault of first impressions, in which her kooky looks were at odds with her height, giving me the feeling she was increasing or diminishing in size whenever she scowled or smiled – though admittedly she *was* tall. Now I knew why I like women that way. I was programmed from when she claimed to be twenty and signed a birth certificate, Helga Johnsdottr. But that Helga was never anyone's daughter.

'You think that is bad Quinton?' she said, bolting the door.

'I dunno,' I shrugged, wondering what the hell we were talking about.

'Let me tell you,' she cast back over her shoulder, mincing past a dusty suit of armour I had first taken to be a drunk old night watchman, slumped against the lobby wall. 'Here in the mountains, you get used to shortages. One week the water is frozen tight. Then rock slides block the road. Sometimes the lightning strikes peoples down in the street.' She chuckled, leading the way along the dimly lit corridor.

'Can you believe that?' she went on, her voice resounding in distant rooms. 'Once, I even loose a *burro* from the hail stones, big as snooker balls they are, always firing out of the blue. Never you know when.'

Despite my resentments, I was warming to her. She was my mother after all. Genes of my genes communicating at a sub-cellular level. Maybe everything would be OK? Sucker thought.

Get it straight.

'... *crocodile emotions with the bite of an asp* ...'

My father's exact words on the subject, the day he came down to my elite boarding school in his chauffeur-driven green Bentley of the long running boards, a car, which, looking back, I loved far more than him. All that came across was cold indifference. Not one question. As if I didn't exist. My mother was a mistake he regretted, ergo so was I. He had done his duty and hoped I would do the same by him. Not many boys had my educational opportunities, and he expected my best. Just half an hour out of his life and, even so, he did not bother to wave goodbye. Sitting very upright in the back seat of the chauffeur driven Bentley, the brim of his black fedora shadowing his solemn brown eyes. All I knew, he was somebody important in the world, but I never found out exactly who. What did I then know about a lodge as old as the hills? I was eleven, minding my Ps and Qs, prepared by matron for the big day, in pressed shorts and blazer. A right pair, my parents. All my life like the swamp fever. Penumbra, impossible to shake off, except with strong medicine, obsessive work and hard drugs.

The devil was high-tailing-it to *las tres hermanitas*, taking the electricity and my luck.

Just as Helga pushed open the swing door and we stepped into the kitchen, all the lights crashed. 'Damn!' she swore into the dark room, the sound absorbed by bare stone walls like spilled ink on blotting paper. 'One day I shoots them down at the station, *mezcal* madmen. They drink anything when it runs out, even the diesel for the generator. Always it is this way. The light goes on. The light goes off. Maybe in an hour it comes on. Maybe never!'

Suddenly her hand shot out. *Madre de Deus*. Those were crocodile claws. 'Wait you and stand where you are.'

Stand in the dark? Hard for dyslexics muddling their lefts from rights. In this case, my horizontal from vertical, or maybe it was the altitude getting on top of me? Just the thudding of my heartbeat and the distant scratchy sound of a croc crossing bone shingle. Africa? No. Just Mother in the next tomb, searching for candles, gloss-red claws scrabbling stone shelves. Mother? I had to stop thinking of her that way. Only one reptile in my family. She was a brood mare, used and abused and put out to pasture. Between us the vast, teeming stockyard of life. The mare who suckled me, seen through a clash of horns, a stranger now and always. Just treat her with consideration, that's all I had to do. She was flesh and blood and bruised easily. A complicated kind of mother who needed tender loving care, just like me.

Yea, sure, carry on trying to warm the iceberg that sank the Titanic. And if, against the odds, I melted that heart, she'd only drown me in her sorrows. She was sad, I knew that, a recluse more walled in than Rapunzel, hiding from the ghosts of her past, shut in this hotel. But she made her choices. I was only five when she left. Why, I might never know. Perhaps she didn't even know. Maybe she didn't care. Well, if she didn't, I didn't. No way would I put up with more shit from that witch. Yes, I'd known exactly who the *borracho* in the bus was referring to when he compared my eyes to those of *la Bruja de la Norté*. Yes, that was my mother, as ever her reputation preceding her, even to these remote parts. But this wasn't Mexico, it was bloody Norway. My mind so far gone, I didn't even know which fucking country. A bad place, this old town overlooked by the three sisters. Fuck's sake, I should never have come.

Light, sudden and awesome, banishing the spooks of the kitchen to the far corners. That flaming wick, vital sustenance more essential than food.

'Here you take, and mind no spills. I have no need for seeing in the dark, not here anyways,' she breathed, her face spectral, under-lit cheeks shining like poisoned apples in candlelight. 'You wait here. I have to put on something ... shall we say ... more coming. So long since I have a real man for company!'

Had she forgotten I was her son already? But then I guessed, it was just her way of intimidating this prodigal bastard, who had turned up so inconveniently. After all, she had a lot to hide, especially from me. So much I needed to know, starting with what had happened to my father *... and his money.*

Stone me, it was cold in the dark kitchen. The only cooking facilities I could make out were a primitive griddle and a blackened hearth, feet siphoning frost from the stone slabs. When the chill reached my heart, I would be an ice statue in

Nifliem, back in the cold kitchen of the old presbytery. Forced to sit still on my special stool, and keep my dancing feet unmoving on the stone floor. Worried Jack Frost might bite off my numb toes, wishing I was a blue bottle fly, with nothing better to do all that long summer afternoon than buzz between the hanging bunches of drying herbs, strung out on sagging lines, where on 'wash Mondays' the housekeeper pegged her ballooning knickers over the old cooking range in the dark, cobwebbed alcove.

Was that a memory? So opaque with the passage of time, the fly was now petrified in Baltic amber? Or an old nursery story about the little boy who ran away, returning to find his mother a troll and his father resting under stone slabs?

Father, are you down there? In your make-do sarcophagus, rigid as ever, laid out with hands clasped to your chest? Keeping close your secrets, fucker.

Nothing else to do but count distractions. Steel in serried ranks, points and milled edges, shining in the gloom. Pestles and mortars, *pequeño* to *mas grande*, reminding me of Rivera murals with large native women pounding the yellow corn.

Pot noodle black now that the flame of my candle stub had finally guttered out. Mother, where are you? Stone, I was stone. Stone cold and unable to think.

Sounds from the netherworld: ragged breathing, reminding I was alive ... from cavernous sinks, a continent away, it seemed, an incontinent drip ... and through the window shutters, an animal retching, that might have been a donkey tethered outside ... Then, announced by a mechanical splutter that might have been a generator starting up, a big basso beat, and a familiar voice.

'*Hickory dickory tock, the mouse runs up the clock. When the bell tolls the Midnight hour, the mouse will be found dead by the door.*'

No, not Daddy, just Vincent Price, reciting the intro to a never released Michael Jackson's track, his coffin-lid tone intensifying darkness palpable as a winding shroud. Midnight? Confirmed by a church bell, striking the hour.

'... *nuevé, diez, once, docé* ...' I spoke out loud, for company, my heart tripping a beat as I counted thirteen. How could that be? Clocks only struck twelve, even in Norway, I supposed. But this was *la Bruja de la Norte's* lair, right? Nothing normal around here. These were the fucking Tropics, for fuck's sake; my nuts were frozen, and this town was getting stranger by the minute. The way I felt, a little bus was still labouring bandit foothills towards a glittering eye on a shining capstone, putting me in mind of dollar bills and treasure, so much treasure, it was piled up to heaven ...

A dream, yes, and so much more vivid than a mere nightmare. I was living it, lost in it, as a high-kicking *bruja* entered, spinning a cocoon of candlelight out of a black void.

'Da-ra-rum-da-ra!' Scheherazade of the *sierras*, back to her *bruja* best, pirouetting purple silks, her powdered face spectral, pouting lips crimson. *Geisha* break. Yep, that mother just materialised. Scary, I'll say. Jezebel could not have looked better ... to a mouse.

Woah ... My head in a spin ... Perhaps my drink was spiked. Locally brewed *mezcal* with a bitter almond aftertaste; Helga wouldn't, would she? I guessed not, sinking back into soft silk cushions of a low white sofa at odds with the stone surroundings, watching her heaping cactus onto leaping

42

flames.

'Another drink?' she said over the snap and crackle of nopal cactus popping in the grate. Dancing flames, casting a carousel of death, in a shadow play of prickly heads flickering across four stone walls, reminding me of a double suicide that now seemed like a sacrifice, the day my life changed forever, my marriage so abruptly ended, and my journey began.

'Oh yes, to the brim please.'

'Oh my *gott*! Quinton, look at that,' she whooped. '*Es muy grandé!*'

The worm. Bobbing belly-up, pink, in my glass, just the way I felt. I'd dragged my slime round the world and up a mountain, only to haemorrhage from the effort.

'You must to drink it up in one gulp,' Helga breathed. Pressing close, her green eyes blurred, turning pyrotechnic in firelight. 'Is good for the manhood, they say.'

'The manhood is not in question, though you are,' I laughed tossing the drink back, trying not to gag as I felt the worm slithering down my throat.

'Now that was not so difficult was it?' she said, smiling. Suddenly she stood up, 'Time for beddy byes,' she clapped her hands, 'Come along now Quinton, I show you to your room.'

Beddy-byes, back in the cradle, tucked in by a Mummy of uncertain size. I liked that, so I rewarded her goodnight peck with a hug which in an instant went from warm to too hot to handle. Yea, and the heat was mutual. No, I didn't want to think about that as I eased out of her clench. Nor of my suspicions. Helga, what nightmares I had of you. The witch ever lurking in my wardrobe. Counting my jackets, picking my pockets – always at the back of my mind as I drifted to sleep. Casting a shadow that only got longer after you left. Mummy, ever absent, always omnipresent. We were friends, I knew that now. Fair-weather friends for the moment. But how long would that hold? Until a change in weather. A tornado twisting down from Texas, spinning a vortex over the high *sierras*.

'You want I should blow out your candle?'

'That would be a relief.'

'Goodnight, Quinton.'

'Goodnight, er, Helga.'

Coffin-lid darkness as, with a click, she closed the door. Faintly the sound of slippers shuffling into oblivion. As I drifted into sleep my last thought directed to the spinner of dreams, not that nightmare please, Sister.

5

THE MASTER OF
SHADOWS

At first I was sure the persistent tapping was knocking on the door. But no, the source was closer. The wardrobe then? No, not that nineteenth-century walnut- burr monstrosity, I guessed was a relic of Emperor Maximilian's ill-fated campaigns in Mexico, with a wooden eagle and a chamber pot on top. How come I missed details like that? Drunk, I supposed, my short-term memory shot. I couldn't even remember getting to bed, but now my senses were on alert, the tapping fading as I struck another match and relit the candle, holding it high, peering into the vaulted gloom.

Nothing, it was nothing. The only spooks were cast by the wavering light of a flame. Even so, I left the candle to consume the darkness as I sank back onto my pillow and descended into the catacombs of sleep..

Something in the room. Before I opened my eyes, I knew. All my claustrophobic nightmares, compressed into one tottering tombstone, incised 'A cynic unknown'. The weights of my nonentity life bearing down, compacting the grey matter in my skull into an ingot of incapacitating dread. Fear was all I knew, and fear was all I had, contemplating mortality in a descending coffin lid, a bottomless grave and a yawning invitation to a dank, green, sulphurous realm. Back-lit, standing in the opening, a figure I recognised - I even remembered his teeth-chipping name -

Mictlan-te-cuh-tli, that same Aztec god on display during my one visit to the National Museum in Mexico City. Only this wasn't a life-size clay sculpture, but the Lord of Death himself, reaching out to grasp me in a skeletal embrace.

As if that wasn't enough, perched his gaunt shoulders, which extended like gantries, a rookery of black birds picking at strips of flesh dangling his rib cage.

And more ghouls looming behind him, too ghastly and too many to describe; these included: Back Stabber, Fork Tongue, Black Dog, Fist Fucker, Blood Blister, Pus Prick, Rubbish-in-the-Corner, Wolf Bane, Crocodile Cunt, Hedge Fund Owl, V.I Paedo-Politician/Priest, Bad Apple Banker, Hag-in-Daz-Nappies, Demented Dick, Huggy Hepatitis, Lizard Lawyer, Bin-Gone-on-Jihad, Born Again Crusader, Black Cap Judge, Persistent Arse-Licker, Miserable Presbyterian Minister, Curious Cop on my case, Wanton Bed-Wetter, of course Pinking Scissor Sisters, Shared HIV Needles, Phantom Brother, Bat Boy, Nosforatu ... The fucking list went on forever. It reminded me how much I hated lists.

My reaction? Reach for my notebook and scribble blindly under covers. Ridiculous I know, but in extremis, the ostrich manoeuvre is sometimes all there is. A warning, I knew, but signalling what? Then a picture filling my mind – a treasure chest overflowing black gore ... a rising blood tide loosing my moorings, my bed now a chariot, harnessed to thirteen laughing skulls, leading me down ... down into the catacombs where, in pitch blackness, native sons toiled with pickaxes and shovels. Another detail I scribbled down as the chariot steadied on its hurtling descent. Had I died, I wondered, as an answer came echoing back from dripping labyrinth walls. 'Not dead yet, but soon will be ...'

My father, sure to god that was my father's voice. *Darth Vader*. Wasn't that German for 'dark father'?

So, the old shit eater *was* dead and buried, somewhere about ... perhaps under the floor of this very room? This town was built on silver mines. Maybe he was buried in one. He might even have been the owner. An ironic twist perhaps going towards explaining his mysterious wealth – never mind what he must have shelled out for boarding school fees and then university before I flunked my degree course and my allowance was stopped. Ten years later I was the only guest in a deranged Mexican hotel run by my mother, wondering if the treasure chest was a figment of my imagination? Those sons of the soil, toiling with picks and shovels, symbolising the mass travail of indentured Indians living out their short lives in the mines below, generations upon generations, all the way back to the fucking Conquest, *and* before, if that date above the door of the hotel was right. A hideous prospect. Because, if correct, I *was* connected; guilt, I guessed, even if only by patrilineal association to a lodge as old as the hills and unnumbered crimes over the ages. For, as it says in the Bible, the sins of the father will be returned unto the seventh generation. Far as I knew, I was the last of the line, successor not just of my mysterious father, but to his before him, and so on, into the mists of time. Whatever was the treasure in that chest – bars of gold, Spanish doubloons, title deeds to the mines or even just my father's bones – was mine by right of inheritance, and that meant I had to take whatever came with it, including all that accumulated guilt.

Only one thing to do when faced with a vastly overweening opponent ... dicker ... parlay for terms ... negotiate a moratorium on heritable dues outstanding. In this case, discover exactly what this Lord Mictlan-te-cuh-tli wanted of me. As surety, offering up my immortal soul, in case I reneged on the deal. For the record, I even jotted the salient details of our contract in my notebook, just in case. When I woke in the morning, I couldn't make out a single word bar my signature at the end. That was frightening. Ridiculous I know to be scared of one's signature, but this is an honest account. It has to be, otherwise I may never escape my present predicament.

6

RESURRECTION?

Resurrection? After my all-night travail, I awoke with a banging bedpan for a head. However, it was still screwed on the right way, though made of inferior brass. Nothing to do but grope towards bumping shutters, weathered wood sieving stars through hairline splits, it was that dried out.

Retinal overload when I threw the catch. The shutters banging back, no window glass protecting against the piercing blast. God-awful Mexico, arid and barren, blowing a gale in my face - painterly slopes, scrub splattered and scree stroked, bisected by a ragged *barranco* - a ravine, from my perspective, more a fault than a chasm, zagging up to where a oversized raptor was perched, feasting on the red fruiting heads of a large cactus. Its pose reminded me of Huitzilopochtli, the Aztec god of war, his double depicted on the Mexican national flag as an eagle atop a cactus bush, eating a snake. Sacrifices on stepped pyramids running blood and *chupacabras* that, in Chicano urban legend, are doppelgangers of an Aztec god, whose unpronounceable name translates as 'smoking mirror of the sun', revisiting the present through a time slip opened up by atom bomb tests in the Mojave Desert. This, of course, unverifiable, unless the monster black bird had migrated south from the barrios of LA and Watts. Still there, perched on the many-headed bush, preening now, big, whatever it was, proving there was no escape, not even in bandit badlands. Yea, wherever I went in Mexico, God, in some guise or other, staring down from smoking mirror heights. In this case on red tiles in abundance, threatening landslides onto narrow streets;

on one flat roof, a heart-warming sight, proving there was life hereabouts, pot plants all in a line, disguised with plastic roses, but still unmistakably Mary Jane. On another, double-pegged washing, near horizontal in the wind. Did I say no escape? There he was come again – Jesus *mix-Mex* Christ – taking it full frontal for mortal sinners, showing the way, embracing the cosmos from the polished limestone cupola of the cathedral gleaming white and pristine under the savage *sierra* sun.

God! Jehovah! Quetzalcoatl! I needed breakfast. I moaned, insubstantial with nothing but a worm for sustenance since the bus station at Chihuahua the day before – and that the hair of the black dog, after the previous night, with whom or what I had already blanked from mind. Perhaps, as my analyst had suggested, my incipient amnesia was self-protective, and I was still suffering toxic overload from primal trauma, suppressed since my early childhood.

Taking stock, I looked around the room, intense white light striking the bare masonry, highlighting dust where stone walls met the old terracotta floor tiles. Then I saw it, scratched on a tile: a hobo sign. Zigzag lines enclosed by an arch, suggesting flowing water in a mine, and below that a box etched with six lines. Might that indicate the treasure chest of my nightmare? Plenty to think about then as, drawn by the aroma of frying bacon, I headed for the salon.

'*Chorisos pequeños, huevos rancheros, tortillas y café, para los dos.*' Helga ordering for us both, addressing a hatchet-faced maid, who gave me a glare as she leaned around the door of the kitchen.

'*Chorisos pequeños?*'

Weeny sausages, for my delectation, Helga said, in a manner that conveyed both disappointment and irritation.

Just the two of us in the old salon, furnished colonial style, window shutters wide to the world. Just wrought fancy Spanish scrollwork and iron bars between us and the hole-in-the-wall *cantina* across the way, where a big man with an apron over a bulging beer gut was swilling last night's slop into the gutter.

'And how do you sleep Quinton?'

The civilities of the morning, I considered sourly, wondering if my *visitation* in the night had just been a dream. What had the Lord of Death granted me? I couldn't think. Oh yea. Six 'intimations', which I pictured as get-out-of-jail-free cards' in a game whose rules I didn't begin to comprehend.

'I asks you a question,' she glowered, swelling ominously. 'And you just sit there not answering.'

'I slept terrible! Not a bloody wink, for my sins.'

'Hmm ...' Helga murmured, diminishing, her attention back to her paperback novel, open on the table; the title, I noticed, *The Eagle Has Landed*.

'You want to know why?'

'If you must,' she scowled.

'A surprise visitation. A ghost, actually.'

Instantaneously, . Helga jerked upright, just as the kitchen door pushed open and the native maid – her bottom half knobbly and knitted, above sultry *salsa* – clacked in on clumpy clogs, bearing a heavy tray.

'Ah, Malinché,' Helga said shakily, lifting her book, making space for the plates. Under the table, her foot pressing against my ankle, bidding me to silence. After maid departed, when the swing door had ceased creaking on its hinge, Helga leaned across the circular table, staying within her size range as proximity allowed, unlike the previous evening when she had fluctuated between XXL and XXXL.

'You have to be careful,' she whispered, 'Or the girls they hear everything.'

'The girls?' I exclaimed, reaching for the earthenware coffee pot. 'I thought there was only one maid.'

'The Malinchés are identical twins.'

'Malinchés?' I reiterated, recalling the maid's sullen look. She'd only been named after the mother of Mexico, who gave Cortez, her lover, the inside track on the Aztecs and so doing sold out her country.

'*Las Doble Equis*, I call them. XX and always looking for a Y. So be warned,' she said, watching for spills on the white *mantequilla* lace tablecloth as I refilled her cup. 'Even I have problems to tell them apart.'

'So how do you do it?' I asked, spearing the weeny sausages. Seven on the fork, and one more; I opened my mouth wide.

Glancing away, Helga sighed, 'There is one that is sweet, one that is sour. What you think, Mr Clever Dick?' She clicked fingers. 'Now tell me what it is you see?'

'Like a flag,' I said, improvising between chews, 'Fluttering, floating and for all I know farting 'til dawn. Fucking evil black shroud.'

'My *gott*.' Helga massaged the worry lines texting her brow. 'Just the same as I see on my first night.'

Slumping, she stared at a point over my shoulder. 'A lifetime ago it seems now.'

'So does every guest get a visitation?' I grinned, 'Or is this an exclusive service?'

'No!' Helga snapped, her prodigious bosom swelling like the boobs of a giant pneumatic Barbie inflating on an airline. 'It is a warning,' she hissed, 'Death, that is the *massage!*'

'Shit,' I choked trying not to laugh, 'That sort of *massage* I do not care for.'

'It is just one of the tests if you are to succeed.'

'Succeed?' I frowned. 'How do you mean?'

'I know what it is you seek. You and me, we are one of a kind. Our blood it is strong. Not like the others,' she sneered, flicking fluff only she could see from the sleeve of her cashmere cardigan.

Now I knew where I stood in her world. Her son, a thing that cried and sucked and then had to be weaned the only way she knew how. Yea, by walking away. Thereafter, a riddle to myself, abandoned in the wide universe for reasons I still couldn't comprehend. But I supposed I should be grateful, given what I knew of her dark past.

Helga stood up. 'We talk more later, when we are sure we are alone.'

She bent close, hissed in my ear, 'And remember not to trust anyone. Most of all that *cabrón*.' She extended a muscular arm about level with my eyes.

'There, you see him?' she whispered, pointing through the window at the hole-in-the-wall across the street. 'Like the black crow he is, looking out from the *cantina*. My *gott*, how I hates him!'

Inflating with indignation, she straightened up. 'That Guzman,' she snarled, 'Always he is spying.'

I was confused. Literally, *cabrón* meant a male goat, yet in the next breath she compared him to a crow. Such insistence, such vehemence. Nothing else to do but ponder the matter while exploring the town whose name I didn't yet know. I guessed I would have to start in the *cantina*.

alcholics Anonymous

7

CANTINA JOE

*C*antina Joe. That's what he said his name was. But the name by the saloon's half-doors was Don José Genaro. Was he not the proprietor?

'Of course!' Joe laughed through yellowing teeth, waving a hand to no one in particular, taking in four walls of bullfighting memorabilia and posters. A riot of red and black, the blood vital and always on a beige background. Vaguely I wondered, why such uniformity? Sandpit life, I supposed, reduced to its bare elements – a crimson cape, a sword, hooves and horns.

'*Es* how everyone around here knows me.' Joe, the universal barman, reeling me in – not at all goat- or crow-like at close quarters, more a greying turkey buzzard, lumps and bumps all over his boozy hooter.

'But Helga said you're called "Guzman",' I said, thumbing towards the hotel, grim and foreboding across the street. Why were the dining room shutters now closed? Did that signal disapproval? Did she see me slip into the *cantina*. Did this conversation rate as betrayal?

'She did?' Joe chuckled. 'A strange woman, my friend.' He winked slyly. 'Who but the north wind can understand her?'

'Yea.' I shrugged, staring into my empty beer glass, scrying strange tales in the thumb prints and froth remaining. 'I suppose that's right. We are all mysteries, mutually,' I offered dully, preparing to go, setting the glass back on the table.

'Even to ourselves.'

'Why the long face my mysterious friend?' Joe clapped my back with a spade hand. 'I feel good today,' he grinned. 'Have another beer, *es* on the *casa!*'

Another beer and another beer. And then overhead the cathedral bell tolled thirteen. Midday? You couldn't be too sure of anything round here, I considered, rising from my stool, regarding my boots shrinking into the middle distance as knees ratcheted unsteadily. Drinking in the morning was definitely not my speciality, hair of the black *chihuahua* notwithstanding. Perhaps I just needed another.

Behind the bar, head and shoulders over the sombrero'd clientele, the three 'mouseketeers' so presented, backs turned, the appliquéd denim of their jackets, chalk stitched and silver studded. A gun, a cactus, a rose. What else? Joe, waving me over, all patent smiles and polished bonhomie.

'But my friend, you only just arrive. In Mexico midday *es* for *mezcal.*'

'Oh no,' I pushed out a palm, 'Not that worm, not at any hour of the clock. *Hasta la* ... I'll see you later.' I shrugged, '*Mañana?*'

'Of course,' Joe beamed broadly. '*Es* no other *cantina* in town. But before you go, *señor, una pequeña, por favour.* Only one *mezcal* – on the *casa, naturalmente.*' He reached for an unlabelled bottle. 'And I promise you no worm. *Es* bad to swallow the local ones, *los gusano del diablo*, the worm of the devil, you know they are called that? The fattest are the worst, especially the pink ones. Always watch out for those. Once you swallow you never lose the craving, they grow huge in the stomach, and always it is crying out, more, more, more.'

'Yea, sure, pull the other one Joe. Try that on the other gringos.' I laughed, not wanting to think of the fat pink worm Helga had forced on me the night before. 'But aren't you going to introduce your friends?'

'Of course!' Cantina Joe gestured as three identical faces, motioned around. 'I am proud to present: Señor Rose, Señor Revólver and Señor Cactus. Already you know their cousins, *las Tres Equis Malinché*.'

'But I thought there were only two maids in the hotel?' I said, turning to shake the hand of Señor Cactus, smiling amiably, and not at all prickly, as I discovered. 'No, you have it wrong my friend,' Cantina Joe said, pouring me four knuckles of *mezcal, sans* worm. 'I should know, for I am their *oncle*. The strangest thing, maybe a world first if it gets into the newspapers.' He shrugged. 'But that is never news in Mexico. Only what is normal in every other country. Double triplets, and both sets identical. A medical triumph only possible by the combined efforts of the United Nations.' Cantina Joe pointed proudly to the UN logos on a plaque above the doors. 'The Canadian doctor in charge says the odds are maybe four billion to one.' He winked slyly. 'I think more, what you say?'

My sort of town, where one and one makes three, and clocks strike thirteen. So many questions. I didn't know where to start.

'Start at the beginning,' Cantina Joe said. '*Es* always the place.'

'Really?' I replied, unaware I had asked a question. *Mezcal* madness obviously. But at least I was feeling better. Fire satiating the worm? I guess.

'So why does the town have no name?'

'Shh.' Leaning across the bar, Cantina Joe sealed sierra cracked lips with a finger. '*Es* unlucky to say, only outside and well away. You have to wait for that story.'

'I see,' I said, unaccountably nervous, suddenly. 'Well then, can you explain why so much of it is rubble?'

'You don't know?' His eyebrows, bushes to nest birds in, shot up. 'Ever since the *revoluçion*, from the four corners, *hombres* packing picks, dynamite and spades. All convinced there *es* hidden here a great treasure.'

'And?'

'Sure *es*,' Cantina Joe laughed lazily, 'The whole world knows of the treasure of the Sierra Madré. But no one ever finds it, for it belongs here, like the *tzitzimime*.'

'*Tz-it-zi-mime*?' I repeated slowly.

'Yes, my friend,' Cantina Joe beamed, 'Like the Condor, only the *tzitzimime* they fly higher. You never get close, except with a spy satellite.'

'Perhaps they're just large vultures?'

'*Zopilotes*, no.' Joe waved airily. '*Mucho* bigger,' he grinned toothily. 'But that was a good try, my friend.'

'The birds are native to Mexico?'

'Oh yes, but only to these mountains. Is the double of an Aztec god.'

'God of what?'

'Thunder, they say.'

'Something new every day,' I said, standing up, 'And that's it.' I smiled, proffering a hand.

'You are most welcome my friend,' gravely Cantina Joe nodded, maintaining an even grip as we shook hands. 'Any questions, you know where to come.'

'That's quite enough answers for the moment,' I said, turning unsteadily towards the swing doors.

8

OEDIPUSSY

Two choices. Left, right and straight ahead. Another instance of numbers not adding up. Even at siesta time the shuttered hotel a definite no-no. Would I ever feel safe with my mother? I doubted it, given what I knew, and that was but the tip of an iceberg. Left then? Towards blackness, an avenue of ruins leading to a sheer face of rock, boss-eyed in the sun, shadows near the summit, caves, I supposed, bordered by two stone lions below, reminding me of Babylon and captivity, guarding the entrance to the tunnel and the world beyond.

Only one choice: follow the pilgrim's way to the staircase wending a conical mound, squared at the base, and topped by the cathedral squatting sphinx-like above the plaza, the whitewashed basilica and cupola tucked in between two bell towers. A head and shoulders guarding secrets, secure between giant haunches.

A question came to mind. 'What goes on four feet, two feet and three? But the more feet, the weaker it gets' The Sphinx's riddle demanded of passing tourists who ended as bleached bones strewn in Sakkara sands. Solved by Oedipus, mother fucker and father killer, blinded for his sins, who still became king, no eyes better than one in that cruel land. The answer? Man. Child, boy and *borracho*. That was me, stumbling worn steps, about to regress to a centipede crawl. Yes! Drunk on *mezcal* in the midday Sun. Father, are you watching?

'Yes, my son,' a voice answered, '*Within and without you, always. In the smoking mirror guarding the gold of the sun. Wherever you look, there I shall be. Waiting for the weary pilgrim on his way to Thebes.*'

Thebes? Could that be the secret name of the town? Anything could be true around here, I supposed.

Now the voice was me, tallying up in a book I keep in my head. How many steps, and each one a hurdle? Near enough a god damn year's worth, I considered, counting three hundred and sixty four. One more to go. Enough to put anyone off religion permanently, I reflected, reminded of the Sphinx and his stupid riddles, staring down at the town; from that perspective like another planet, alien and odd. Impossible to think it was inhabited. Formerly the richest town in Central America, with a theatre where the Paris Opera once played, a treasury where bullion was stored, a government mint which issued gold pesos, and a population of around 70,000, not including the indentured Indians forced to work their whole lives underground in the mines, only seeing the light of day on Sundays when they attended mass at the cathedral, according to Wee Donald. A hundred years later, only the grand old buildings of the cobbled main street were still standing, and most of those derelict. Spiky desert plants sprouting upper walls, pediments, turrets, gables. And there, at the tunnel end of the main street, a scything shadow, sweeping red tile rooftops. Yes, that big bird again, same as before, just a fleeting glimpse of black feathers, swooping down behind one of five rock pinnacles, like the fingers of a raised hand, jutting the cliff wall that enclosed the town on three sides.

Heat on my back, then cold, that cloud a smoking mirror guarding the gate to the sun, reducing my choices to zero. Before me, the truth, the way and everything else Catholicism stands for. A door within a door, and a handle on that door, like the ring pull of a hatch on an ancient hull.

Noah's Ark maybe? Another native legend according to Wee Donald, one of the mountain hereabouts, where it finally grounded. Myth and legend of the Sierras, smoke and mirrors for the credulous. At that moment I could have believed anything, staring at the high arched wooden door, bordered by stone impedimenta, the seven deadly sins; pride taking a fall, gluttony sleeping on the job, avarice with his head in his arse, the snake of envy coiling a harlot's thigh – or was that lust? I didn't know. All I could see was lust for life in the rutting skeletons and intertwined serpents, chiselled in life like detail around the great arch of the doorway. Or were those snakes just *mezcal* worms? And fuck it, those concentric carvings, were obviously modelled on the nine circles of Mictlán, meaning that this cathedral was also a pagan temple, which reminded me of long evenings in the New York Public Library, boning up on Meso-American burial practices. Well, I was studying for an anthropology degree before I flunked out.

Nothing else to do but take that penultimate step; plunging in, temporarily blinded, as my eyes adjusted to the darkness within, feeling my way round the screen like the *borracho* I was, secretly ashamed but going ahead anyway, crossing myself dyslexically and again, reversed – just to make sure – waiting in the gilded gloom, waiting for dancing noughts and crosses to add up.

Clue one to two hundred and twenty. An anagram for suffering: wounds gory, a bloody pincushion, except those were arrows and that was wood. Now I got it. Martyrdom, glorious to behold, Saint Sebastian on a plinth, staring sullenly. One saint down. How many more to go? They were all round the basilica, snug in niches, imminent and transcendent on wires as performers in a circus – the congregation of the saints according to papal edict. Or maybe not, I thought, noticing Gregor, the saint of drink, and his famous St Bernard; neither recognised by the Vatican for seven hundred years. There were even some fallen from grace elsewhere, St Boniface, the protector of children, leaning on his broom; St Christopher shouldering a lamb; St George, twisting his spear into a life-like worm, a saint dismissed as a myth by the Vatican council of 1910, but still believed in these mountains. Mad Catholicism, at its most perverse, gilded in gold leaf. I loved it, and I hadn't even penetrated the inner sanctums – confessional boxes, screened by frayed red curtains.

'How long has it been?' my confessor asked, after I got down on my knees, unable to resist baring my soul. An Irish brogue, cosy as Spanish fleece, Paddy-whatever, Einstein hair silhouetted in a grill.

'Father, I can't remember, it's been that long.'

'If you take a moment for reflection. There's no hurry, my son.'

'"My son ..."' What I'd come to hear, trust the Irish to provide honeyed words. 'Father, I have to confess, I'm not even a Catholic.'

'T'at's a new one on me, I must say, but the Church is as wide as the world, wider if you need, my son. There is room for all.' He paused, and I felt a fluttering within– my heart a fledgling bird. Perhaps I was a Catholic. So much of my early past a locked box, anything could be true.

'Somet'ing you need to get off your chest?' he asked helpfully.

'Yes. No. I'm a dyslexic fool and liar for one. Or is that two? I'm so confused, Father. For all I know of my early life, I might even be a Catholic. And yes I've had lustful thoughts. You see my mother is a very attractive woman. We've only just met after many years and she doesn't yet know who I am. I think we're in danger of forming an incestuous relationship, Father.'

'The devil comes in many disguises. Are you absolutely sure she is your mother?'

'I am.'

'Well don't you tempt her with the worm, it could be her downfall. And being a loving son, you wouldn't want t'at?'

'No, most definitely not, Father. And yes, despite everything, I do love her.'

'Love sometimes comes all too easy, my son. It's separating the flesh from the bones, t'at's the t'ing. T'is old cathedral sits on a pyramid of bones. Did you know t'at? Not just any bones, my son, the bones I'm talking about are the bones of Indians sacrificed on the old pyramid on which this blessed cathedral stands, dedicated to Tlaloc, a name which means "the germinator". Each one a martyr to that pagan deity. What do you t'ink they cry out for? Justice? Revenge? Absolution, more like! Bones is your inner core, my son. Bones is your forefathers, all the way back to Noah. And the ink that joins them? Sin! Incest! Fornication! Patricide! You name it, they did it. It's all in there, my son. Reflect on bones and you'll realise the transience of life. All else is vanity, my son. Vanity!'

'So that's what I've got to do when I get the, ah, urges. Think about bones?'

'As a matterphorically speaking, yes. It's a hard one, I know, but t'at's the way, my son.'

'Any special sort of bones I should think of, Father?'

'Thigh bones, hip bones, they're all much of a muchness, my son. It's the marrow you've got to get to, the core of the core. The pip of the pip, so to speak. Only the other day I was reading in *Scientific American*, you know, the ah ... scientific magazine, all you are is encoded in your marrow. Now isn't that a wonder! Genes, that's the vital substance, you must understand. Even in the bones of ancient Egyptian mummies, they're finding it, and some of those mummies are soon to be regrown from the marrow out. Proving there is hope, even for the worst cases. To t'ink that Ramses, the pharaoh who had a run-in with Moses, could soon be as alive as you and me, walking, shopping, doing ordinary t'ings like that, makes me t'ink that the End Days are close at hand. Remember the Scriptures my son, when the last Trumpet sounds all the dead since the beginning of the world, six t'ousand, six hundred and seventy-five years ago, to be exact, shall be raised. Now wouldn't that be a sight worth crossing the Liffey for.'

The Liffey? I was in Mexico, not in a snug in a pub in Dublin. I'd come to confess, and now this garrulous Irish priest had taken over my starting stall and was off and running. Geneticists? Moses? *The Last Trump?*

'But Father,' I protested, a vast oppression coming on, 'What do I do about all these sins?'

'What sins was that?' He really sounded like he'd forgotten.

'I guess all the way back to the Garden,' I said, succumbing to temptation. 'My forefather monkey believing his cousin's heads were apples.'

'Now t'at's a most interesting theory, my son. Would you care to expand?'

'I didn't come here to talk about *Scientific American*, or genetics, or Genesis, I just need to confess, Father.' I paused, becoming aware I was wringing my hands. 'But what ... I don't recall.'

'When you do,' he soothed, 'Just come back to the Cathedral. You will always be welcome, my son. You have my word on that, and I don't give it lightly. If I'm not here, one of the other Black Friars will confess you.'

Black Friars? Now I knew I was in trouble. Unwittingly I'd poured out my heart to a Black Friar 'Shemite'; a renegade sect of priests, accused of double heresy – denying Jesus Christ *and* assimilating Native American beliefs into the Catholic liturgy – who were now the subject of a secret Vatican commission, as covered in a recent edition of the *Notional Enquirer*, my favourite tabloid. That 'certain somewhere' in the Sierra Madre was here. In a place that, by not having a name, had one, as the capitalised letters of the Town With No Name, demonstrated, in the article. As if its existence was tantamount to nonexistence, and both states were interchangeable and confused one for the other.

New meaning on old bones then. That priest laid a lot of stress on old bones. And I hadn't seen a single crucifix in the cathedral. More to this than meets the eye, I thought, returning to the hotel in a pensive mood.

The Notional Enquirer, *Issue No. 12633. pp. 12*

POPE ORDERS CRACKDOWN ON NASTY HABITS AS MAD MONKS GO NATIVE

By our special religious affairs correspondent, Poop-a Snooper

Rome. Tuesday 23rd July 2013. *New Pope Sixtus V has convened a secret Vatican commission to look into the habits of the 'Shemites', a breakaway sect of Black Friars who deny virtually the whole Catholic liturgy, Jesus Christ, the entire New Testament and indeed all the books of the Old Testament after the Book of Noah, with the exception of the Epistle of St John the Divine. The heretics claim that ancient Native American texts uncovered in the sacricity of an unnamed Mexican cathedral have revealed we are merely mutinous survivors cast adrift on a spinning disc of dark matter, acting on our thoughts as a magnet does to iron filings, orbiting by a smoking mirror otherwise known as the 'fifth sun', which is positioned between man and God. The Shemite brethren, or 'Eagles', as they address each other, are preparing for the 'second coming' when the final 'sixth sun' will consume the earth in a great conflagration in a remote fastness in the Mexican Sierra Madre, where the 'pilot', Shem, son of Noah, apparently known to the Aztecs as 'Tlaloc the Thunderer' will arrive in a space ark, to return the self-appointed 'elect' to their home the planet Æden, which lies beyond the solar system in the constellation of Pegasus. Vatican sources attribute these heresies to 'vitamin deficiency caused by a meagre diet through a lack of funds down to the parsimoniousness of their congregation, prolonged altitude sickness and an excess of religious zeal, particularly self-mutilation'.*

9

THE VOICE

So, the *wonderer* returns.' Helga, posed in the doorway, busting the buttons of her designer dungarees, barring my way.

'You want chapter and verse; where I've been, what I've done? Really, Helga,' I sneered, 'You sound like my ex-wife.'

'Do you humiliate her like this also?'

'Yes,' I winced, 'I mean no.' I shook my head in an effort to clear it.

'What do you mean?'

'You asks me that? When I sees you falling out of the *cantina*, crawling like a cockroach up the Cathedral steps.' She scowled, towering over me. 'You stink of mezcal!'

'What if I do?' I jawed.

Helga arched a plucked eyebrow. 'I asks you to stay away from the *cantina*. I am your mother. Do not I deserve a little respect?'

'I might respect you more if you hadn't abandoned me when I was five.'

'So it's about that? You know nothing.'

'You'd be surprised what I do know, *and* remember.'

'Ach,' she shook her head, 'Just like your know-it-already father.'

'And he abandoned me too, the fucker. Don't forget that. Where the hell is he anyway?'

'Do not swear. I already tell you we talk later.'

'What's wrong with *now?*'

'I do not get any sense from you when you are drunk like this.'

'Oh God,' I groaned, 'Helga, you are such a nag.' I said, observing that the pencilled lines of her freshly denuded eyebrows precisely followed the contours of the previous incumbents, making me wonder why she had plucked them in the first place. Women, I thought, you never really know them.

'I only nag you because I care for you, and I know the dangers of this town,' she said, checking the empty street in both directions. 'Come!' she gestured. 'We needs to talk, but first you must change your clothes and scrub up. Your trousers, they are filthy; look there is dirt under your thumb nail.' Her lips curled. 'My *gott*, so disgusting you are!'

A night and a day, not even twenty-four hours, if the cathedral bells were anything to go by, and already we had arrived at this station. Clearly there was no other direction but down. My poor father, who could blame him for casting her out? At least he had come see me at boarding school, even if only once; Helga never had. I felt abandoned all over again, watching her stride up the corridor, out of sight but not out of mind, round the corner at the far end. No one to share my thoughts but the 'old retainer' – the dusty suit of armour – back against the lobby wall, stiff and unyielding, impervious to the insults of women, enigmatic under his helmet that demanded to be set straight.

'There,' I said, taking engraved Toledo steel, in need of a good polishing, between my hands and easing the dusty helmet into a more upright position. 'That's better, isn't it?'

'*Much better.*'

The *voice* was back, this time resounding the narrow

confines of the lobby. Jolted, I looked behind, and then checked the corridor ahead, but it was empty. 'Father?' I said, peering under the helmet at the black void within, 'Is that you?'

No answer. Just eyeless hollows staring back. Under the helmet a mummified, toothy corpse, pale cheekbones protruding bitumen skin.

'You like him?' Helga said, suddenly appearing over my shoulder. 'My favourite man in the whole wide world,' she pouted. 'Never he gets drunk. Never he talks back. Always doing his duty guarding the front door.'

'But, who *is* he?'

Helga shrugged. 'What does it matter? I buy him from the Black Friars. Plenty more under the cathedral. Always they are coming up in the cemetery. They are buried one on top of another, many of them pilgrims, who come here to kiss Shem's sacred shin, and never return. You see them stacked at the side of the cathedral. Nothing rots in these mountains, something to do with the dry *sierra* air, they say.' She smiled winsomely. 'The armour suit,' she sniffed, 'It comes with the house. Spanish, five hundred years old.'

I was back in my room, but no escape there.

'*You ask me if I am your father.*'

'Now I suppose you're going to tell me?' I groaned, rolling over on the straw mattress of my bed and staring at the wall.

'*Yes, I acknowledge your claim. Forefathers, how many generations? Seven to the power of seven? At least that – numeracy never a strong point, plenty of scribes around for that – the house of Inkenhaton, a many-branched tree, rooted in the rich mulch of patricide and incest.*'

'Just what I needed to know.' I moaned, pulling the pillow over my head. 'Fuck off you old fucker.'

'*A noble lineage of how many twists and turnings, all the way back to the Deluge and before,*' the voice droned on, '*A fine boy, one any father could be proud of, but the cause of much current concern. My former consort is the problem.*'

'You mean Helga?' I interjected. Throwing off the pillow, I noticed a large spider, motionless in his web, high on the wall under a roof beam, over by the window shutters.

'*She has many names, and is always making forbidden ends meet. Her way of avoiding the cut, self-renewal and all that. Incest, supping from the smoking mirror ...*'

'Smoking mirror?' I said, wondering if a sudden buzzing in my head signalled the imminent materialization of this phantom, who I didn't really believe really was my forefather or an ancient Egyptian, before realising the sound was only a large blue bottle fly tangled in the spider's web.

'*The steaming liver of her unredeemable double ...*'

'How can a double have a liver?' I demanded, as I watched the fly's struggles weaken.

'Oh, they do, most certainly, my son, they are used for augury at the sacrifice. White lead of the sky in that cup, self-love and eternal gratification, all the way down the line.'

'And what line is that?' I said, as the spider scuttled a gossamer thread over the dark canyon that was my room.

'My line, my son,' he said, as the paralysed fly gave up the ghost. 'Like a predatory nuthatch she is burrowed into my wood, always emerging to nip-off the best buds soon as they reappear. She, knows, of course, who and what I am, that's why she keeps me captive in this armour, so blisteringly hot in summer, so perishingly cold in winter, but I never blister and I never perish, would that I could – a prisoner at the gate, my manhood cut off at the root and kept in its sarcophagus, held by a cord, the knot secured by an unbreakable spell given her by the Witch of Endor, another fiend. Always a stickler for detail my ex-consort. Presentation and paying close attention her special talents.'

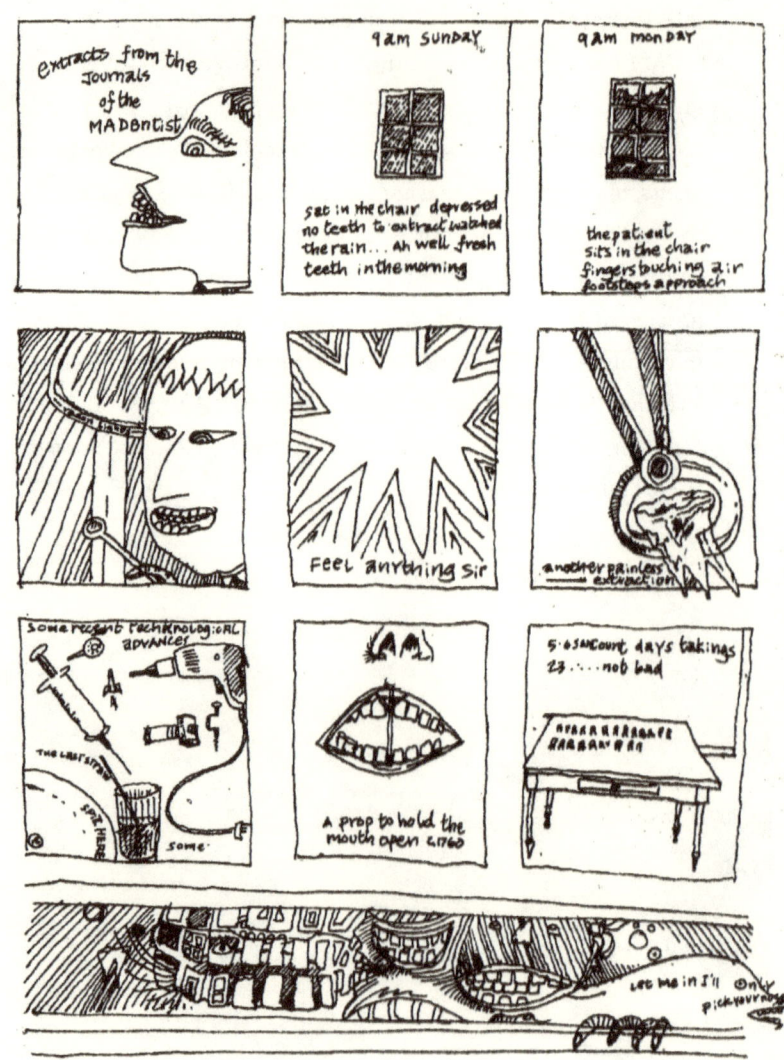

10

GREEN BUTTONS ...

We needs to talk. Her words still ringing in my ears. Even so, I was putting off the moment, trying to ignore the sudden onset of toothache. Lying, stretched out on my bed, holding a hand up to a candle flame, staring at four fingers of my left hand glowing red in the gloom. Just like I used to, I realised with a jolt, accompanied by a jabbing pain in my jaw. Forget that I told myself as, unbidden, a memory surfaced of that never-never land of lost childhood: hiding out in my den under the eaves at one end of the attic in that rambling old Presbytery. The cisterns gurgling, every time downstairs a tap ran or a toilet flushed. Above my head, jackdaw scuttling the slates, higher, a crow cawing from the chimney pots, another from a branch of the whispering trees over by the garden wall. Below, a bishop pacing the boards of his study, the same old board creaking every time he circuited the Bukhara carpet. *No let up from the toothache.* Forget that. Instead, try to remember the scent of the spring blossom on the whispering trees, sounds of the housekeeper at her chopping block by the coup in the courtyard at the back of the scullery, where the concrete's stained around the drain. A chicken squawking in her giant grip, poor wee thing, no escaping that great hand. The squawks cut off, when the axe strikes the block. It's time finally come, as the Bishop would say. *Shit, this fucking toothache is getting worse.* Chuck it over the high wall of the front garden, where I wasn't allowed to play on Sundays, onto in the cobbled street beyond, where the Knife Sharpener, is on his rounds, this being Thursday morning. Whirling the mysterious gears of his barrel, set up on the pavement by number 9 next door, sharpening Mrs P's shears. The screeching sound, making my fillings vibrate. Yes, I had them even then, every week, dragged by the housekeeper to the mad dentist round the corner, getting my teeth drilled. That was the way, then in the old country, when a common 21st birthday present, was having all your teeth pulled and replaced by false teeth, to save the future expenses of dentists, who had a drill in everyone's mouth, it seemed when I growing up. Fucking dentists. That Thursday, the neighbours, were waiting their turn to get their knives sharpened. Women mostly, never missing a chance for a natter, a few men in line, including the rich dentist from round the corner looking embarrassed. Kids playing. Yes, the kids I wasn't allowed to play with, because they were common and I was posh. A well of tears, where a white snake circled turgid waters. The glint of treasure, down there, the paleness of bones too, lots of them, tossed in, on the passing. A poisoned well, where once sprang cool clean water. Them bones. Too many of them down there. All sorts. Chicken bones. Clavicles. Plastic skeletons from cornflake packets, that glow green in the dark. And drilled milk teeth, rejected by the tooth fairy, from under my pillow. Yep, me – self-realised Shemite, Catholic, whatever I was – just as a confessor abjured me, meditating on bones, pip of this pipsqueak and all that. But I would grow withered before I penetrated those secrets, I thought wearily, far better to ask....

Think of the devil and the devil always appears in some guise or other.

Yep, that was the second time that day.

Oh, it's you Helga,' I attempted a grin, working myself up on my elbows on the bed, wondering why she was wearing a short red dress, that started mid-thigh and ended mid-cleavage, instead her everyday dungarees, posing in the open doorway, with one naked knee cocked like that.

'Come on lazy bones, get up,' she clapped big hands, 'I make a fire in the Salon. Everything it is cosy and nice for our little chat.'

'Please, can't we put it off till tomorrow Helga,' my grin turned to a grimace– I needed out of this. That dress it was just too tight, the satin riding up her slim shanks, knockout legs. Fuck's sake, that was my mother. 'I've this terrible toothache. It started up when I got back, and it's just gotten worse and worse.'

'You have mercury amalgam fillings?' she asked.

'What?' I sat up, shocked at her intimate knowledge, then realized of course she knew, she'd been the housekeeper at the Presbytery, all that time ago.

'I asks you a question, and still I am waiting. Please make the effort to answer.'

'Yes, I do as you well know, I have lots of fillings in my teeth. I fucking hate dentists.?'

'Must you swear.' She sighed.

'I'll try not too. I promise.' I said, holding my jaw.

'Ok. I tell you. It is because the altitude here in the mountains it makes the metal fillings swell up, and that is why your teeth hurt. In a week or two it settles down, silly boy.'

'A week!' I moaned slumping back on the bed. 'A fucking week!'

'I tell you not to swear,' she said, inflating.

'I didn't mean to, honestly the word just popped out. Go on please.'

'Ok, the teeth they gets worse before the ache it gets better. And before you asks it is a week minimum Quinton. I see the same many times with visitors to the town.'

'Have you any medication, please? Something stronger than aspirin or paracetamol?' I said hopefully.

'What I have it is much better than pills.' She laughed, gaily, 'The local remedy for any pain in the head. It is a-perfect. I promise you will like.'

'That sounds good, but please Helga I don't want any of your horrible herbal potions. I haven't forgotten you know.'

'Don't be such a cry baby Quinton. I guarantee this it will be right up your alleyway.'

'Up your street ...'

'What!' she snapped.

'The correct expression is *up your street* Helga.'

'Ach,' she snarled, stomping off, 'You are so like your know-it-already father.'

After a minute, Helga returned with a small wickerwork basket filled with what on first sight looked like green buttons.

''What are they?' I said suspiciously, looking into the basket, she held out to me.

'Peyote, I get them from the local *curanda*. She gets them from Hutcholi Indians, who hunt the cactus at night in the desert below the mountains.'

'Really? They hunt the peyote?'

'Yes, with spears, to them the cactus is a sacred animal.'

'I see.' I said, puzzled. 'And how should I take them?'

'You put in the mouth, suck, and they keep the pain away.'

'I have always wanted to try Peyote, but ...' I hesitated.

'Go on,' she encouraged.

'How many should I take?'

'Four to each side inside of the mouth should be enough.'

'But I don't know if I want to get stoned right now."

'For the drug effect, you have to take twenty or thirty.' she laughed, 'A few buttons just numbs the gums.'

'Seriously?'

'Quinton, you need to trust people more. I only offer them to help.'

11

THIS MÖBIUS
MEXICAN REALITY

Commotion in the salon before a big fire of nopal cactus. Helga toasting marshmallows on a stick.

'More mooshmallows, my dear?'

'Nope.' I shook my head, 'the sweetness doesn't mix with bitterness of the Peyote, frankly.' I said speaking thickly, through the wad in my mouth.

'And how are the teeth now?'

'Quite numb thank you. It's better than novocaine.'

'That is good.' She smiled. 'So you wants to ask me questions.'

'Yes,' I nodded, wondering where to start.

'About?'

I swallowed, gagging on astringent peyote juices, 'I guess the first one is, why did you split up my father?'

'I do not know if this is the best time to answer that Quinton.'

'There never is a best time, Helga.'

'You are right,' she sighed. 'If I have to spill the whole pan of beans, that is what I must do.'

I nodded, finding her quaint English amusing. Pan of beans indeed. Couldn't even get that right, my kooky mother; she was lovely really.

'All my life Quinton, men trying to make me. Maybe because I am tall, they feel they must to. You know, I get in some hell of a scrapes. Your father tells me he saves me from sin when he offers me the job of houseweeper.'

'Ha,' I laughed, that's a good one. 'Carry on.'

She frowned. 'As I say, he employs me to be his houseweeper. At least that it is what he tells the visitors. But the good times in the old church house do not last. Soon we are fighting over the names he calls me from his Bible. Jezebel. Delilah.' She paused, hang-dog. 'Harlot, always harlot.' She looked up. 'Do you know what this means? Always I am wanting to find out!'

'You really don't know?'

'Why you think I asks?'

'Prostitute,' I sighed.

Her green eyes gleamed. 'My next job in Hamburg, always with sailors making spurt from every port.' She shook her head. 'Always they are telling me this.'

'But what happened to my father?'

'There is a scandal.'

'What about?'

'Me! Who else? He blames me when the newspapers write he is living in sin with his Houseweeper, and throws me out. He is a Bishop, and for him sin it is not allowed.'

'Yea that follows,' I nodded, finding it hard to speak with my mouth numb from the peyote.

'You know, it is strange.' She settled back on soft sofa cushions, conjuring a face with a languid cast of a hand. 'In a way you remind me of him.' She sighed. 'Nothing physical, you understand. He was, how you say, sallow and short, where you are fair and tall like me.' Frowning, she looked away. 'Maybe it is how you move.'

'Ok, so that was the bishop.' I said, irritated. *No way was I like that holy prick.*

'Perhaps we should start at the beginning? Like where you were born.'

'Why don't you tell me since you are such a know-it-already.'

'Fair enough,' I nodded, 'Let me see, 'You were born on an island.'

'Now you are fishing.' Helga swelled ominously.

'No,' I shook my head. 'Not a guess.'

'How it is you know then?'

'That would be telling,' I smiled.

'You are making me angry now.' She glowered, and I hoped she wasn't about to pop. But she wasn't a balloon. Not with that face of rock.

'If you really want to know,' I dissembled, 'It's all to do with semantics. The world over, island people phrase their words in a different order than mainlanders.'

'Why do you not tell me this in the first place?' she said suspiciously.

'Maybe I didn't want to bore you,' I shrugged. 'I can get quite pedantic on the subject. At university I took a course on word order in colloquial dialects, but most people don't find the general area interesting.'

'Hmm, you are right,' she nodded. 'Too much study makes Jack a dull book, I always say.'

'That is because you are an islander. I bet when you were young you were always out of the house exploring.'

'How you know that?'

'Because on a small island, kids are that much are easier to find. I take it the island was small?'

'Not when I am young, it is a universe then.'

'A very small universe,' I laughed, finally at my ease with this big busty blonde, who, for a moment at least, I had forgotten was my mother.

'It is exactly on the Arctic Circle, or was when I left.'

Pausing, she raised an eyebrow. A cue, I knew, but I merely nodded.

'Just like this town is on the Tropic,' she continued. 'Is that not strange?' She smiled, reflectively. 'On the shortest day, we can see the sun over the horizon. There is a tall mountain with three peaks they call the three sisters, cows in the fields below and many, many trees.'

'Really?'

'Yes,' she nodded, 'We have mountain ash, hawthorn, pine.'

'So far north? I find that surprising.'

'We have the Gulf Stream to thank. It is no colder than here. We even have apple trees with beautiful golden apples.'

'Sounds like a mythical garden.' I lofted an eyebrow. 'Only in the wrong place.'

'That it is true, but in summer the sea is not so cold,' she smiled, diminishing again. 'And sometimes on the beach we find Malacca beans.'

'From the Yucatan, I suppose,' I chuckled.

'Why not?' she frowned, inflating slightly. 'The Gulf Stream it starts there.'

'So it does.'

She sighed, deflating, 'Everything on the island is so beautiful.'

'I am sure,' I nodded. 'Whereabouts exactly?'

'Either you guess right or not at all,' she glowered, swelling again.

'Sorry,' I said, already informed that the island was one of a chain of three, some three hundred nautical miles due south of Spitsbergen.

'So many questions,' she pouted, stabilising. 'But that is enough Quinton. I am tiring now. We talk more over breakfast in the morning. '

'Promise?'

'I do not repeat myself Quinton,' she growled, and pointed a finger at the salon door. 'Now be a good boy and go to bed.'

The old ghost from the lobby was back, his scratchy voice loud in my head. 'What do you want?' I said, snapping into wakefulness, lying on my bed in the shuttered room.

My son, you are in danger.

Son, he said *son*. I had to know. 'Is this my father talking?' I demanded.

'*Only in the sense I founded the Inketaton line of which you are the last AND most miserable example.*'

'You are the founding forefather?'

'*Yes.*'

'You are not a demon?'

'*This is no time for discussion, my son. It will soon be dawn, you must leave the house before the cock crows.*'

It was in my mind. My research. This conversation. This hotel and mythical treasure, which Wee Donald believed was buried, in a mine hereabouts. The *cantina*, Joe and all the mad *borrachos* across the street. The heretical Black Friars up at the cathedral. This möbius Mexican reality where everything ended up before it began, here in the town with no name at the end of the tunnel. Yes, this was just a primal scream therapy session gone wrong and I was back on my analyst's couch having a nervous breakdown – that was all. Obviously, mine was a classic case of projection. My analyst had morphed into another father figure, in this case, the lobby ghost, who clearly was suffering from Alzheimer's since he was fixated on me, believing that he was my forefather. Since my divorce I projected onto every strong male personality I came across, including Wee Donald. Perhaps the fears my analyst had dredged from my unconscious were the thwarted desires of my beastly inner child. One day I'd find the key to unlock his cage and let him out to vent his rage and spleen against everything unfair that had happened since he was first locked up. And stop blaming my parents, who had their own reasons for abandoning me. Helga wasn't the *Bruja de la Norté*, she was my mother and friend. I was just having trouble with the extreme nature of our mutual attraction. Considered rationally, such a planetary pull was not uncommon between mother and child reunited after a separation of many years; otherwise everything was quite normal.

'Please leave me alone,' I said, pleasantly as possible, addressing the lobby ghost again, 'I don't know who you are, or rather were, but you are certainly not Ancient Egyptian, nor my forefather as you claim. I have come along way to find my mother, and I am not, repeat not going to leave the hotel on your say so.'

'*You young fool. Why did you not do as I say? Blood of my blood, I ... I ... dis...*'

Just then, from outside my window, a cock crowed, cutting off the lobby ghost mid-sentence. It was dawn and all I wanted to do was sleep, far less talk to Helga. Jesus, how the hell had I ended up in this haunted hotel. Stupid question. Perhaps I just needed a fucking break ...

Sinking back onto the bed, I noticed the window shutters were outlined in rainbow colours. Obviously the peyote was stronger than it had first seemed. The colours were really nice, and I felt floaty, so I reached over to the basket on the bedside table and took some more.

12

THE BRUSSELS CONNECTION?

Helga looked up from her paperback novel, as I entered the Salon, 'Good morning Quinton,' she smiled, her green eyes, larger than ever framed by her reading glasses.

'Morning Helga,' I mumbled, slumping into a chair, wondering why formality. Something was up.

'I make you breakfast today,' she said, closing her book, replacing her glasses in their case, and rising from her seat.

'Can't the Malinchés do it?'

'I give them the morning off.' She half turned towards the kitchen, 'That way it is safer for talking. *Húevos rancheros?*' she said brightly.

'Na,' I shook my head, 'I'm not hungry. I didn't sleep much. I think it is the peyote. But I could murder a strong coffee.'

'I also hardly sleeps two winks Quinton,' she said, pouring me a mug-full after she had brewed a fresh pot. 'All the night long I am tossing and tossing.'

'Our late conversation was that heavy, huh?'

'It is not so much that as thinking of things I should tell you.'

I leaned closer, 'About what exactly Helga?'

'Your father, and how I meets him.' She sighed heavily, looking diminished on the other side of the round table.

'Yes, I would like to hear about that.'

'Quinton, I fear to tell you, it is shameful.'

'You know what they say,' I smiled, 'A trouble shared is a trouble halved.'

'I hopes so Quinton.' She nodded, 'I hopes so.'

'I am all ears now.' I said, waggling them with my fingers.

'I know you try to cheer me up.' She half smiled, 'You are a good boy Quinton.'

'You'd better believe it.' I beamed, basking in the attention of my long lost mother.

'You know your father he is quite right when he calls me harlot.'

'You were a prostitute when you met?'

'No, Quinton, that was before.'

'You were a madame?'

'Ah, that is the word I am looking for, yes. The money it is much better. And you know who I works for?

'Search me,' I spread my hands, flummoxed by the turn of the conversation.

'For the Swedish Minister of Defence himself. My official title is senior manager in Human Resources, though I gets the job because after I leave school I train as a nurse in the Swedish Army.'

'Go on,' I encouraged.

'My job is to inspect prostitutes and make sure they are clean for our clients from arms fairs. It is in the course of this work, I am told to recruit thirty blonde girls for a very prestigious club in Brussels.'

'Hold on. I thought this was in Sweden.'

'At the time we have a legation with the European Union, where my peace loving country sells a lot of arms.'

'So that's explains the Brussels connection.'

'Your father he is an important member of this club.'

'Tell me more.'

'The club it is very old. They claim it is started by Charlemagne.'

'Seriously?'

'Hitler he is a member too, I see his portrait on a wall, and other famous heads of state, royals, aristocrats, and wealthy men. Many of these men they are supposed to be enemies, and you find they are all in the same club.'

'That figures because of what they have in common I suppose. So what are they all into?' I laughed, 'Don't tell me it's brussels sprouts'

'No,' she shook her head, 'Not vegetables. They eat shit.'

'What?'

'You hear what I say Quinton.' she scowled.

'So, it's a copraphiliac club?

'Yes that it is the word. The condition they say goes with ultimate power. Only in that club they only eat the purest shit from the whitest asses served on solid gold plates.'

'And that's where the blond girls come in?'

'You pick up quick, Quinton. Yes, they are fed but nothing but apricots for one whole month before the ceremony.

'Why?'

'Because that it is the length of the human body waste cycle. After twenty eight days all that comes out the other end is apricot residues, nothing else. But first, all the girls they must have a medical procedure to qualify, and even are glad to take it. For the ritual, they are supposed to be virgins, but the club secretary knows this is impossible in the day and age, so he pays to have their hymens reconstructed, in a private hospital.

It is a simple procedure, and the girls are treated very nice like they are on holiday. Then at the house, they are not allowed out for the whole time, but for that they make a lot of money, and earn many favours, also, because these men can make anything happen. Some girls they even gets married to the men.' Helga smiled.

'So, what's the ceremony about?'

'They are calling it the Golden Apples of the Sun.'

I frowned, 'That sounds familiar somehow.'

'You hear about before?'

I shook my head, 'Probably it was something else. Please carry on.'

'At midday on the Summer Solstice, all thirty men sit at a long table, each with a solid gold plate, a knife fork and spoon also solid gold on the white tablecloth before them. One by one, the girls, all naked, walks out from behind a purple curtain, at the end of the table, like it is a catwalk. They each squats, deposits a golden offering on a gold plate, and leave. Only then the men they eat, with the gold knives forks and spoons, taking tiny bites, and chewing very slowly. No one says a word, it is all very serious.'

'Oh, that's disgusting. Yuck. So what had my father to do with this?'

'Always they have a bishop to give the blessing. That year it is your father. And that is how I meet him all that time ago.'

'So was he a secret shit eater too?

'He had his strange sides, Quinton. Better you do not know about that.'

'I've heard quite enough today about that holy prick.'

'And I too do not wish to think any more of him.' She smiled wanly, 'More coffee? I make another brew?'

'Yes, please. And a couple of slices of toast would be good.'

'You want breakfast now?

I nodded enthusiastically.

'That it is good, for there is something else I want to talk of which I do not wish the girls to hear.'

'So, what's it all about? I said, after I had eaten, pushing my empty plate away.

'I need for a partner.'

'A partner?' I sat up straight. 'What for?'

'I think you know already Quinton.'

'So, remind me Helga,' I grinned. 'Since I am such a *know-it-already.*'

'For the treasure of the Sierra Madré, hidden here in this house.'

'Yes, I have heard talk about that.' I said, remembering Wee Donald's words on the subject, 'But if it really is here, why do you need me for Helga? You are in charge.'

She frowned, inflating slightly. 'Quinton, you must to understand, I am a woman alone. Even if I finds it, that it is only the beginning. I still have to get out of the town alive. So many dangers,' she thumbed over her shoulder in the direction of the Cantina, 'Guzman for one, always spying. The girls in the kitchen for another. And now we have a new problem.' She grimaced, 'I get a massage today. Gomez, the owner, he wants to sell up. Not enough business, he says.'

Another dark chapter, in an unwritten book. *Pride and Prejudice* and Gomez. Her first lover in Mexico, a man of the *mestizo* under-class, climbed the greasy pole of ambition in the only profession then open to mixed bloods, becoming the police chief of the region, before taking up a senior position with the federal police in the state capital. Hated in the town on account of his ten-year reign of torture and terror, envied for the fortune he had made from the drug trade, and facing certain death if he returned. That was the reason Helga needed me to go see him and find out how advanced were his plans to sell the hotel.

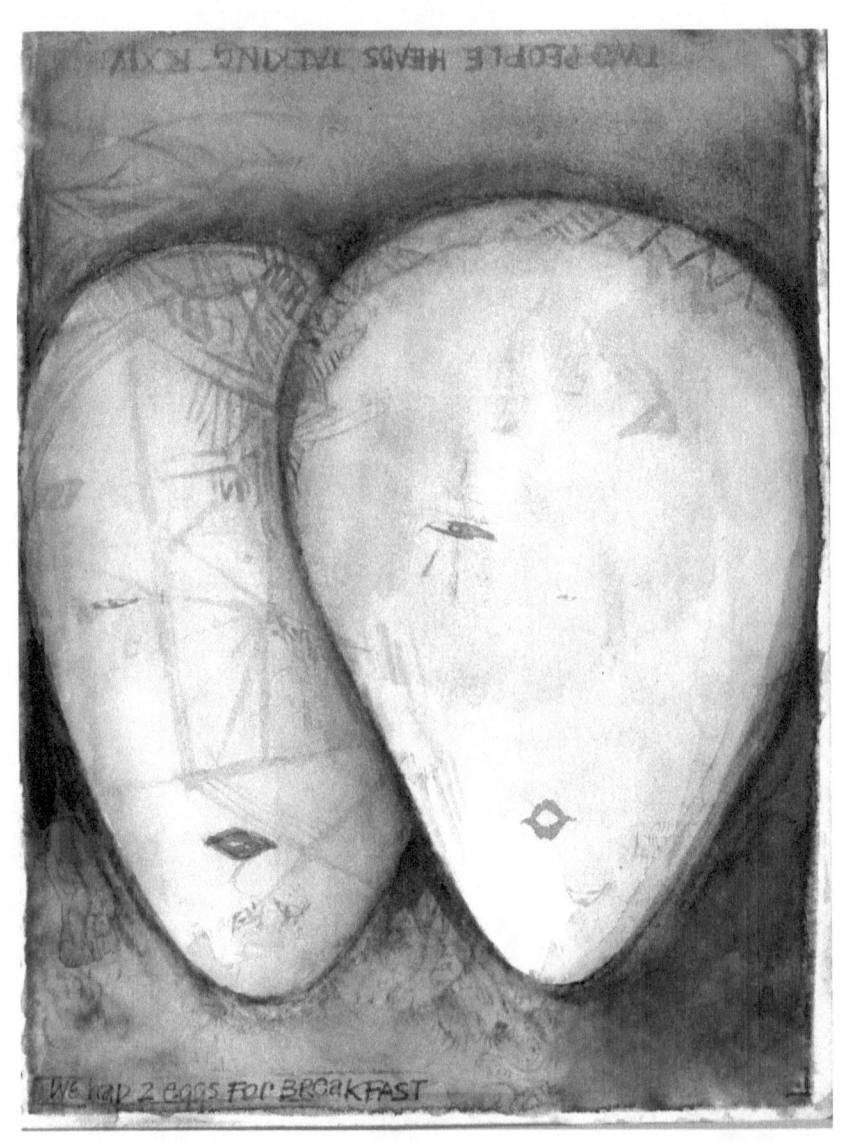

13

GOLDEN YOLKERS

Good to get away, boarding the little bus. I had a lot to think about as I set off into the tunnel, treasure mostly, and our Q&A session over my late breakfast.

'Liss'en,' she hissed, 'Gold is shit, it attract a lot of flies.'

Yea, I liked that. So we were the flies. But where was the ointment?

'Shit is like gold, it makes a smell.' She tapped her nose. 'And I can smell it somewhere close.'

Nice one, Helga. I could hardly contain my *huevos rancheros* – double yolkers, golden apples of the sun. Was she sure it wasn't the drains?

'No, is true! Big drains under the hotel. Like the catacombs of Rome down there. Mine-es for miles.'

'Surely not?'

'Oh yes! All the short-life miners down on their knees, get born, fuck and die! Here were the richest min-es in Mexico. So many bones for the priests. Indians of the mountains, and the plains for hundreds of miles around too forced to live the whole life underground. Men, women, children, only those that convert, allowed to see the light on *Domingo* after Mass. Each carrying as much ore as they can balance in the palm of one hand. All their wages to build the cathedral.'

'How long did that go on?'

'Since just after the fall of Tenochtilan.'

'Not sixty years before?' I said, thinking of the date carved on the front door lintel.

'No.' She shook her head. 'Seven years after. Thirteen

conquistadorés, hunting the last of the Aztec eagle knights in the mountain forests, camp down for the nacht. In the morning, a black slave who gets the name Ventura notices silver in the ashes. Where they make fire is the mother hole.'

'Mother hole?' Laughingly I interjected, 'Don't you mean mother lode?'

'Hole?' she snapped. 'Load? For some mothers is the same. Soon all the trees are cut down cut down for pit props, and the land as far as the crow can fly turns to desert. It is men that do this, not women. Three hundred years later they are still mining, so much silver there is, the street outside it is cobbled with ingots, their descendants still ruling the show. But then comes Pancho Villa and *la revoluçion*, the silver cobbles from the cathedral to the tunnel are dug up, and the Spanish owners they pay for the bullet, taking to their graves the secret of where they hides their fortunes.'

'Ah, the treasure,' I grinned. 'Everything leads back to that.'

'Of course.' She nodded slowly. 'Why else you think this house is called *Castillo del Dinero?*'

'Any idea where it might be hidden?'

'You see how thick the walls are.' Frowning, she looked around. 'Three, four meters.'

'No.' I shook my head. 'There'd be signs of disturbance in the bare masonry. I've checked all the walls. You can't hide that. I think it's deeper. Perhaps in a sealed-up mine?'

'Why you say that?'

'Just a hunch,' I dissembled, careful not to breach the terms of a deal struck with a diabolical ally, who I was counting on coming good in the future with get- out-of-jail cards – whatever the six intimations were.

'Maybe you are right,' she sighed, looking away.

'Why the sad face?'

'Sad?' she shook her head, 'Not me. I am just remembering a story Gomez tells about skulls blocking the drains when he is changing the house into a hotel.'

'How many?' I demanded, a sudden tingling on the back of my neck, suggesting the demon of the treasure was listening in. Was there ever any escape from my fears? I guessed not, at least within the confines of the hotel.

'Thirteen,' she shrugged. 'Miners, he said, from the old days before *la revoluçion*.'

'How did he make that out?'

'From the style of the tools his builders find close by.'

'Pickaxes?'

'No,' she scowled, her mood downshifting and her size swelling accordingly. 'Adzes, the same as the miners they use up to the eighteenth century.'

'But why just their skulls?'

She smiled, 'An old belief, separate your enemy's head from his body and he cannot haunt you.'

'There could be another reason. Like they knew where the treasure was. They might even have buried it and that's why they were killed.'

'Of course that it is possible,' she inclined her head, 'But I don't think so.'

'Why you say that?' I demanded, a voice in my head, telling me she was lying.

'The treasure is hidden when the town is under siege by Pancho Villa, and not before, when those skulls are buried.'

'But thirteen skulls, in this building? Come on, there's got to be a fucking connection – and I don't mean Belgium!'

'Around here,' she shrugged, 'Thirteen is not many. Why,

only a few months back, they are finding maybe forty skeletons under the bandstand Gomez builds in the plaza, before he leaves the town for good.'

'From revolution times?'

'No,' she smiled, 'Much more recent. Ten years ago Gomez he is brought in as chief of police.'

'Why, when there are so few people living in the town?'

'To stop the drug traffic.'

'Is there much round here?' I said, wondering if she knew where I could score some grass.

'Do you not yet understand there is no money in anything else in this country?'

'Yes, of course,' I nodded, that voice in my head again, telling me this was not the right time. 'So what was his problem?'

'A tribe of albino Indians that the legends say are still hiding out from the *Conquistadores* in these mountain somewheres!' she laughed. 'Yes, Gomez really believes a white tribe is growing marijuana in a secret canyon. He is searching for them, when the fool crashes the governor's helicopter into a stupid thunder bird.'

'Thunder bird?' I laughed.

'Yes, yes, sometimes in thunderstorms, you see them high in the mountains, when lightning strikes. As I say, they are just big stupid birds. Gomez never finds the canyon, because it is a story in a book he read by an idiot Belgian, and so he makes an example of the next pueblo, where the people are selling the marijuana. But then he goes too far, even for his friend the state governor, who only gets elected because he always turns a blind eye. There is even a report of the massacre in a national newspaper, and calls for an inquiry, though of course nothing happens. That is why he can never return to town and wants to sell up,' she laughed, gesturing towards the hole in the wall cantina across the street, 'Too many of Guzman's relatives out for his blood.'

'He sounds a right cunny funt,' I muttered dyslexically, jolted by a roseate glow pulsing her midriff. But then with another jolt, again my viewpoint shifted and the glow was all around. I was in a veined red cavern of living flesh, pulsing boompty-boom, the glowing walls creeping with pestilential black ferns.

Then, equally abruptly, my viewpoint shifted, and I was back staring at Helga across the table, wondering whether I had just experienced a womb memory.

'There is nothing to worry for,' she smiled, to my considerable relief, back to default size. 'I tell Gomez you are my friend, and he will respect that.'

'I hope so,' I said, realising that I had just received the first of my six intimations from the Lord of Death – suppurating black tendrils revealing, in graphic detail, that she was eaten up with cancer. It was just a matter of time. Perhaps she sensed her time was soon up and she was bound for Mictlán and that was why she was sad. But at least I had found her before she kicked the bucket. Horrible thought, and a crying shame so it was. Better she didn't know, she'd only shoot the messenger, or *massager*, as she would call it. Poor Helga, whatever plans she had would go awry, I knew that now. For myself, I had undertaken to go and see Gomez, which is what I intended to do, come hell or high water, because my mother had asked me to, bless her black heart.

14

CASA LOCA

So that was the conversation, and now for the view. The bus belching out of the tunnel, black fumes clearing on cactus-buttoned *mesas*, cross stitched by tracks and snaking with roads, freightliners grinding down on donkey carts and Cadillacs – the high plains bisected by atlas biceps – *cordilleras*, ranging north to south, corded knots knuckling a map, mounting as far as the eye could see. The top of the world from a Mexican perspective. A strange feeling, as if I'd entered a different dimension – not the last time I'd experience that sensation – the Town With No Name, a ghost in more than one sense, misting up in memory, making me wonder if I'd ever existed back there.

But this was my world. A world of colour instead of the monochrome of the mountains, where it was warm instead of freezing and you could buy newspapers, and pass the time without worrying your nuts might freeze off, waiting for your connection drinking coffee at the bus station kiosk. Glad it was caffeine, and not peyote, firing up my system. No problem with the teeth, at the lower altitude and consequently no more peyote delirium either, thank goodness.

A hell of a kick, that newspaper picture. Real life out there. Gangsters and cops battling it out. '*Arriba México!*' The punchy headline, '*Cacería Humana*'; in plain English, 'man hunt'. Man hunts man hunts man ... was ever it not so? At least that wasn't me. '*El numero uno narcotrAficante*' – even I had heard of Jaime Everrardez de Léon – 'Robin Hood' to his pals,

111

on the run after blowing away a US DOA agent, I thought, in dyslexic mode again. Or was he a DEA agent? My eyes had gone funny in the half-light, same difference either way, the world had moved on and another soldier bitten the dust. Nice one, I thought. I never liked the feds and their rule book anyway. With every new entry the walls of the world closed in some more.

But this was Mexico, where but one law applies – all depending on who you know, what you know and maintaining a poker face – comedians and *gringos* excepted of course. The foreigner was easy meat for any Mexican pointing the finger. Under Mexico's Napoleonic code of law, a simple *j'accuse* is enough to get you extradited or indicted. Another of Helga's cautions: don't try to bluff out cops. Especially high-ranking federal cops like Gomez.

Plenty to ponder then as, in falling twilight, I made my way to the bus stance, to the head of … what queue? A novel experience in Mexico where the masses go by bus. Pulling in now, a *Primera Clasé* space liner, royal blue curtains tied back on vacant portholes, sleek and burnished excepting the tarmac-bitten tyres and scrapes attesting to donkey carts pushed off the road. No conductor for once, only a highway bandit for a driver, grinning as he opened the door, jacking *zapata* eyebrows as I announced my destination.

'*¿En serio señor?*' Like he really meant it. But then, when I asked if there was a problem, he shrugged with the coded message, 'What did he care about *chingados gringos* anyway?' He'd take my money anyhow. Even more to ponder then, as we set off into the real blue yonder.

Plenty of scheduled stops to mark time by; after five lay-bys and still no takers *el capitan* abandoned the three-lane highway

– as good as I'd experienced in Mexico – raising plumes over the chaparral, taking a dirt track short cut, cross stitching the barbed wires of cactus plantations, agave stretching to sandbagged desert defences. A no-man's-land now consumed in dust, as we climbed into the stronghold of night; sentinel pines guarding the passes, timber-tops cresting the high ridges of finger-lickin' sugar-frosted stars gone patchy with mist; the bus defying all known laws of gravity as we descended, shuttling switchbacks, the driver intent over illumined dials, his face console-green, *el capitan extraterrestre* flying by the seat of his *Star Trek* pants.

Even the atomics of the seat I was gripping, with a tenacity born of vertigo, seemed in doubt, careening in a bus out of time and out of this world. Brought back to earth by the jewelled splendour of the city blazing into view below, a fire-fight of topaz dragons and peridot boulevards locked in immortal combat, all the way to the glittering prize – *el céntro* – high-rises and hoardings, a tiara garnished with emeralds, sapphires and rubies, competing with the stars. Let there be light! Man in abundance, banishing night with his flares.

Did I say abundant? A gross error. The bus' broad windshield, a panorama onto desolation. Where were all the *mariachi* bands? This the best hour to be plying their trade, serenading *borrachos* stumbling cantina doorways, all closed now, as were the shuttered shops. Perhaps a national hero had died? But that would mean firecrackers and fusillades, a funeral was never a dull affair in Mexico. What then? Mass pestilence to explain the absence of *tamalé* vendors at street corners? Hardly. Food poisoning not an issue south of the Rio Grandé – for many dysentery a way of life. And where were all the squeegee monkeys, prosthetic clowns and brain-dead fire eaters parading backed-up traffic at intersections? All gone ... along with the courting couples, the promenaders, legless skateboard beggars, the dispossessed and befuddled huddled in doorways ... unfathomable mystery, as the bus jumped the red lights, the driver as good as blindfolded, all the way to *al céntro.*

Perhaps we'd crashed back in the mountains – this bejewelled city a necropolis of the dead; waiting at the bus station Aztec morticians with obsidian knives separating the incorporeal from the weights of tiresome flesh. A long queue back there, given the poltergeist population.

No one, just no one. No taxis and no payphones, but plenty of morticians skulking the crumbling concrete halls, sliding into slatted shadows whenever I turned. Nothing else to do, but start walking; one direction as good as another, I supposed, faced with threading underpasses to nowhere, or climbing buckled barriers onto spaghetti flyovers – and that no use, all the roadside signs plucked for roofs in the nearest *barrio,* misdirecting crows and low-flying aircraft. Nothing makes sense under harsh neon, everything a metaphor and all ultimately untranslatable; those close-grouped electricity pylons screened by high wire, Angor Watt in quarantine transported from the jungles of another Siam, that corrugated assemblage framed by scarified scaffolding, a slice of Black Forest gateaux fit for a hobgoblin king straight out of Brothers Grimm. And what about that stepped square of gravel by a city block-wide excavation? The Pyramid of the Moon, where nightly flayed bodies were consigned to the pit, stone chips settling, spookingme out as I walked by.

A car! One of those cruising sedans I'd spied, but only at a distance, either at the next intersection, or slotted between

114

tall, earthquake-cracked buildings. How come they were all two-tone and the same *marqué*. Fleet cars, I suppose, confirmed as one neared me. Police pheromones I can smell at a hundred paces. I needed no sensor to realise here were heavy cops.

Gomez was a cop wasn't he? Nothing else to do but hitch a ride. I know how to brass the case when all else fails – and wasn't the car stopping anyway?

'*¿De dondé eres?*' My heart beating faster, rasped words, drawing a bow across over-strung sensibilities.

'*No hablar Español, señor.*'

True, my Spanish deserting me at that moment.

'Ah!' In the darkness of the car's interior his grin was a glint of gold on an otherwise blank page. 'You *Eeenglish* tourist?'

'Yes. No.' I nodded then shook my head, hoping that way to confuse them. 'Not exactly. Just visiting. My uncle actually.' Randomly I pointed to the Grecian colonnades of a large mansion, partially obscured by cypress trees set out like traffic cones, gracing a nearby hill. 'He lives somewhere in that direction, I think.'

'*Es Méxicano*, this *oncle* of yours?'

'*Si, señor*,' I said into the open car window, giving the script to the four blank pages arranged about the seats. 'Maybe you know him, for he is an important man in the federal police.'

The name Gomez: a magic carpet to satellite dish summit, where I found myself before the ornate but stout panelled door of a rococo pink villa, columned in the Doric style, at my back canine heads on plinths, commanding a sweep of rosy marble steps, leading down to a driveway that artfully snaked parking cone cypress trees and Greek statuary to a big black hedge and no-nonsense high-security gates, behind which the police in their car were watching as I pulled on a repro antique bell chain, drawing a chorus of celestial chimes. Verdi on tap, the 'Rite of Spring', drowned out by barking, as the front door flew open on a lanky stick man, all angles and interstices, in tow to a black brute of a Neapolitan mastiff – a breed of dog I recalled was favoured by the Camorra.

'Señor Gomez? I'm a friend of Helga's', I said, wondering if he was a cappo of the Camorra in on the Belgian connection, looking askance at the dog's drooling jowl, paddling paws and straining lead, which was chewed in the middle and linked to a spiked metal collar, by a cheap looking clasp. 'The name's Quinton,' I said, rattled, 'All the way from the bloody Serengeti,' I added with a grin, recovering.

'Serengeti?' he frowned, then sat-nav references seemed to slot in place. 'You better come in then,' Gomez said, clearly impressed I had come all the way from Kenya. 'Bruno,' he mouthed, kneeling to earwig the brute, pointing a long finger, his bloodless lips nuzzling black velvet. 'Es amigo. Friend of the family. No biting now.'

So I was now included with the 'family'. Could it be that Helga's stories of a bishop were a smokescreen, and her Mexican lover was my real father? I would still have been born a Catholic. But no, I thought, checking out daddy-long-leg genetics, I came from a higher order of life, and besides, no father of mine could be a cop – particularly not an Indian-murdering cop like him.

'You come at a bad time.' Gomez cast back over a dandruff shoulder, his blue blazer flapping, gold buttons glinting, his shirt tail hanging. Bruno padding happily ahead, leading the way along the pink hall decorated Versailles-style, between cut-crystal etched glass mirrors reflecting uncertain futures, and gold cherubs aiming arrows from porphyry plinths inset in the gilded frames. 'A very bad time,' he said again, flinging open a tall mahogany door.

There goes a man of action, I thought sourly, watching him eat up the carpets in attenuated strides, his heels clicking on parquet by bay windows draped with a makeshift assortment of brocade, sheets and blankets quite out of character with the designer look of the room. He headed for a ghastly monument to bad taste that occupied a good portion of the far wall: Tutankhamen's cocktail cabinet in diamond dust lacquer, striped gold and black, complete with horns and wings, the boy pharaoh looking down on a splendid selection of drinks. Gomez refilled a glass with Napoleon brandy, drenching it in ginger, before remembering to ask what I'd like.

'Johnnie Walker Black Label,' I replied crisply, settling into one of several sofas, deciding against Chivas Regal, the only other blend available. I was reminded that, when it comes to whisky, the world over, the rich, know next to nothing about malts– in Scotland the preferred choice of courtiers and paupers. No bar without a selection, and most smaller than that effete faux-Egyptian cabinet.

Johnnie Walker it was. Another man with long legs and alcohol for innards, I thought sourly, watching Gomez reach for the awkwardly placed bottle, a ladder and a crane for anyone else, strain showing on his pasty long face as he turned. He handed me the bottle and a glass, telling me to please myself, loosening his tie and sighing loudly as slumped in the opposite sofa.

'*ChingAda puta madré*,' he swore to no one in particular.

'What, *my mother?*' I snapped.

'No!' he replied hotly. 'Just *chingAda* every mother except your mother, if that's the way you want it. What the fuck do I care? All *putAs*, always shopping and making men pay for restaurant bills, and babies always more babies filling up the world with more assholes. I hate this life, you know. Hey!' he sat up, not caring that he had just slopped drink on his Armani slacks. 'I forget you name. So sorry. You must be wanting to show me the brochures.' He clutched his head. 'A lot on my mind right now.'

I smiled, confused by his mention of brochures, then, recovering my aplomb, jumped up and bowed in the Prussian manner, which I hoped would impress him. Hand on heart, I announced, 'Quinton Moriarty, at your service.'

'Quinton?' His eyes widened. 'You are not Quinton from the travel company?

You are from the hotel, the joker Helga tells me about?'

'She did?' I said, pleased somehow.

'Sure,' Gomez said, breathing easier, 'She text me every day on the mobile ...'

'Really?' I interrupted, 'I thought there was no signal in the mountains?'

'There are base stations for military communications.' He shrugged, 'You know Helga and her connections.' He unbuttoned his shirt collar. 'But yesterday I tell her, no more.' He shook his head, looking like a mop on a pole as his lank hair showered fresh dandruff on his blazer. 'Not now they have the number.'

'Who has the number? I demanded, quick as a shot.

Gomez tensed. 'What does it matter, who? Cops for cops,' he choked, wiping spittled lips with the back of a hand. 'Worse,' he continued, '*Gringo* cops for *Méxicano* cops.' He gestured wildly towards the heavily draped window. 'One thousand in the city tonight! *Con permiso de la pinché* NAFTA agreement. They can go anywhere with all the back-up they want. Mexico is a country no more,' he wailed, pressing spider fingers to his temples. 'The *gringos* can do as they like with us.'

'Is this about drugs?'

'*Comó no?*' Gomez said. 'When that is seventy per cent of the trade with the States. Everything else is alfalfa,' he sneered. 'All the players, north and south, have a piece. Ever since Reagan, with the US budget deficit now stacked past the moons of Jupiter. Operations those Congress fat asses, pretend never happen, paid by what we bring over. As my confessor at the cathedral called it, "*la mano izquierda de la obscuridad*" – the left hand of darkness wiping the shit in secret places. A sad fact of this shitty life, my friend. That is why I cannot understand this disaster!' Hands deep in trouser pockets, he stood, perhaps seeking confirmation of his continuing existence in the black shine of Italian shoe leather. 'Maybe is because of the exchange rate,' he muttered.

'Come again?' I said, wondering if his confessor was a secret shit-eater. Father O'Flattery, I was sure. Could he really be a member of the most exclusive club of all? If so, it was an ass overhead inside-out underworld.

Gomez sat down beside me on the sofa. 'In my country, you must understand,' he said, 'All serious *négocio* is in dollars. And for that you have to pay the black market rate. Is like a tax on the people, eight maybe ten cents above the official rate. But recently that changes. The same *narco trAficante* who ices the sacrifice, like kills the *gringo* agent,' he shrugged, 'Starts the war when he sells cartel dollars for pesos, and undercuts the official price. His trade is so many billions it

119

drops the dollar ten cents worldwide. Now the Chinese are panicked and jumping out of US treasury bonds, which are propping up that Jupiter-high junk pile of bills, meaning that *mañana* the dollar could be confetti.'

'Bad fucking scene,' I said, connecting all this to the newspaper report. 'That is fucking heavy.'

'You are right my friend.' Gomez clapped my shoulder. 'And this is the wrong place.' He stood up. 'Is a bad time, a very bad time. You must leave, *now.*'

I was about to protest this was not at all a good time, what with all the heat about, when came a thunderous banging of the front door – hideous barking too. Bruno sprinting from behind the sofa, the lead snagging his master, towing him by the heels, drink arcing as Gomez skidded to the floor, taking a rug with him, out of the room and down the hall, ploughing a furrow in the marble tiles.

'Gomez, you *pinché* fok!' said a man's voice, pitched to make himself heard above the din of door chimes, barking and banging. 'For the love of God,' he cried in a falsetto. 'Let me in!'

15

TRAFICO ...

Call it instinct, second sight, whatever you want, but I knew who was banging on the door. As the paper said, 'El número uno narcotraficante'. Forget Sid Vicious of the Sex Pistols, Elvis Presley, Tupac Shakpur, or any such impostor. This was the man himself. My ultimate hero.

And here he was, Jaime Everrardez de Léon, ably assisted by a palpitating Gomez. And what a prince of the Tulullan blood - Cuhuatomec's line of course- of the order of valour. Well, I'd have given anyone an award dressed like that in body-hugging Lycra, bar-coded black and gold, diamonds studding playboy shoulders, more on his fingers; his sallow pencil moustachioed face was just as I imagined d'Artagnan of the Three Musketeers, small but perfectly formed - only more handsome, if that was possible, saturnine with flaring nostrils, quirky bushy eyebrows juxtaposed at angles, and below ... such danger in burning black opals, staring directly into mine. It came to me then: I would die for this *hombre*.

'Who the *fok* ees that?' Jaime shrieked.

My all-time hero fingering me? *J'accuse*, in an out-thrust hand, impugning me of unnameable crimes, innocence personified on the sofa, supping my whisky, any residual coolness down to my state of shock. That just could not be.

And then I realised, Jaime wasn't pointing a finger or any such extension, in his steady hand, aimed at my pounding heart, was a small revolver. Pearl handled, from this low angle.

Wait a minute now, I ain't no gringo foker. I'm a friend ... your best friend if you'd only believe me. Words I wanted to say, dying on my lips. The divide of the conquest between us, as I met Aztec obsidian eyes, and all that happened since.

'Gomez tell him I am OK. For fuck's sake man! Before it's too late!' I pleaded, momentarily ensnared by panic. The red-hot tableau forever branded – Gomez stranded high and dry, his mouth opening and shutting like a pike out of water, Jaime exuding deadly force, his finger curled on the trigger.

Time for a diversion. 'Second thoughts, Gomez,' I grinned, 'Why don't you tell Jaime that joke about the pie, the cook and his sticky little fingers?'

'What the fok you saying man?' Jaime frowned.

'It's really funny,' I insisted. 'Go on Gomez! Don't be a party pooper.'

'What is this foking joke?' Jaime hissed.

'I *fogget!*' Gomez tore his hair. 'I don't know any such joke.'

'Make up yo' mind!' Jaime's eyes bulged.

'Put the gun down,' Gomez snapped, back in control. 'Quinton is family. *Un hombre de honor.* You can trust *heem,* even as you trust me.'

What a recommendation. Something to write up in my CV. Jesus, I didn't even know who I was, only that I wouldn't play the sacrificial victim. No one could lay that penance on me. Not this pilgrim. I'd see them in hell first. Well, maybe. Jaime had *múchas próblemas muy grandes. Número uno,* the ring of steel, corralling the city. *Número dos,* the night curfew. *Número tres,* his image flashing on TV news bulletins on the hour. *¿Número que?* I just lost count, his *pistoleros* either shot dead or getting the third degree, gonads wired, sweating gigawatts under bright lights. Most of all the five million peso reward.

Who could he trust with such a price on his head. Who indeed? I wondered for the umpteenth time, checking out Gomez, on a marathon, wearing a track round the carpet, calling up associates on his mobile, his hand clamped to his ear, urgently speaking gangster euphemise.

'*Chingon*! Turn the sound down, I cannot hear!' Gomez swore, pointing towards the plasma TV and Jaime on his knees, chain snorting from a beaded little nose bag, channel hopping, entranced by his YouTube image repeating on news bulletins.

His face red, Gomez slammed the phone on the smoked-glass top of a gilded coffee table. 'Is no use. The whole town shut tighter than Porfiro Diaz's sphincter! Every way out blocked!'

'No,' I said, swaying slightly, over by the bar pouring my third Chivas Regal, down to my second choice after drinking steadily through the night. 'Not every way?'

'Fok! What you say?' Jaime, for the first time in hours showing a different side than a bobbing Lycra ass, as he turned away from the plasma TV.

Whisky, ambrosia of the gods! Accept no imitations or adulterations, stay on the amber trail, and you'll always return full circle, eventually. The rule applying even with blends. That third Chivas had quite cleared my head, all the clouds rolled back off the heather.

Jaime was small, even petite, I pointed out, no insult intended. If we plucked his eyebrows, shaved his moustache, dressed him in a blouse and skirt, gave him discrete tits, and applied lipstick and mascara, anyone would take him for a woman. No curfew had been announced for daylight hours, and who would suspect a *gringo* and his *muchachita*. Of course he would have to practice the hula, swinging his hips, but I had been coached by the best, so that would be no *problema*. For delivering Jaime through the ring of steel, best achieved by mingling with the masses – a dreadful prospect for someone so refined, I knew, but of limited duration – it being my certain experience from travelling round the world, buses are only cursorily checked at roadblocks. As for a refuge, both Gomez and I knew somewhere that, to all intents and purposes, was out of the world, so fucking obscure, it didn't even have a name.

I had almost forgotten my purpose, why I had come to *Casa Gomez* in the first place; to plead for a stay of execution and leave off selling the hotel. At least wait 'till we found the treasure. No, I didn't mention that, but I thought of it, watching Jaime smacking lips – in love with his reflection, Scarlet O'Hara posing in the bevelled hall mirror, hands on hips, winking at me. What a sweetie. I was entranced.

'Is too late,' Gomez replied, his eyes hard on mine. 'Helga sold it to me in the first place, and did not exercise her option to buy it back, so I do not understand why you have to come. However, only last week, after *muchas negociaciones*, I exchange it with a small contribution towards my pension, lock stock and wine cellar *por un pequeño Castillo* in the Pyrenees,' he smiled disingenuously, 'Or somewhere like that.' He rotated pasty hands, reassembling castles in the clouds. 'Even harder to find than the hotel.' Flaky eyebrows emphasising the point. 'All through intermediaries. But I can tell you, he is a high-ranking diplomat and a member of the very best clubs. Belgian?' Fingers taking a walk, scratching his scaly scalp. 'I forget!'

Shit-houses, I thought, at this latest reminder of a

connection best forgotten. Not another colonialist on the make.

Gomez approved my plan, but only after he had proposed a couple of '*poco*' alterations. The last stage of the journey, as outlined, was simply too dangerous. 'Mountain Indians' were not like city folk, too self-preoccupied to see beyond their noses, they possessed a sixth sense, he insisted over Jaime's loud guffaws; in the close confines of the little bus, his disguise surely would be penetrated. Some stupid *borracho* would start feeling him up and that would be that. But there was another way. An old *burro* trail fallen into disuse, the only option long before the tunnel.

So it was to a bus and a train, and then ... but I was getting ahead of myself. Perhaps the most dangerous stage of our journey was before us. The long walk to the bus station.

'*Wok?* You out you mind, man? Never, in my whole life!' That was Jaime's one protest before we started. But then Gomez pointed out taxi drivers all were radio connected via cab-central to police headquarters and, like the mountain Indians, possessed an acuity that stripped bare all pretence. Quite a thought that, I considered, a sense of power and possession taking a grip, as I took Jaime's delicate little hand into mine.

16
HEADS OR ...?

By bus and by train into the night. Standing-room only in the unlighted third- class carriage, shuffling with menacing moustaches, as matches flared in the sullen crowd – *clandestinos* heading *norté*, gathered in silent contemplation. New prince of Bel Air or a prison cell and the bum rush back? Or perhaps just glad not to be with their *compañeros*, clinging to the carriage roof above. But my thoughts were mostly directed through the open but barred windows, wafting sweet scents of ... jasmine? Boletus cactus? I didn't know. The only certain thing the knotty outlines of the shadowy *sierras* tracking our clanking progress, the eye of the hunter Orion, winking balefully where jagged peaks scratched the stars. At last the familiar outlines of the three sisters and our stop, a lonely *estación* in a bleached vastness. No platform, just a drop onto drifting white sands that silted a shot-out sign pointing towards the mountains – and the town, I hoped. A string of bullet holes rendering the legend all but unreadable, only one word legible, '*Catorces*', in faded letters, the paint cracked and peeling. Another nameless mystery to ponder as we set off.

Easy enough following Gomez's crudely drawn map, navigating the desert by starlight, following a trail of rotting carcasses and the gusting stink of shit to a vast and deserted pig farm, marked on the map, at the foot of the mountains. Skull and cross bones signs warning of the dangers of swine fever on its high perimeter fence, which was busted outwards as if by a stampeding herd; we skirted it to where the path divided before a low mound covered with the gnarled roots of a most singular tree. Closer at hand, a stone stele, about a meter high. On the nearside, a bas-relief of a bearded wayfarer with his staff, pointing to a weatherworn inscription that might just have been cuneiforms, though it was hard to be sure in the shade of the looming canopy above. The huge half-dead oak, last survivor of the great forests once swaddling now naked slopes, forked by countless lightning strikes. Old? Bloody ancient. Ancestor spirits, congregating twig thickets, rustling the great girth of the trunk, which, on closer inspection, I saw was hollow and charred at the base, as though burnt out by a hobo's fire.

'Which way, man?' Jaime demanded in a grating – now all too familiar – whine. And again, when I didn't answer, he just turned and stared sullenly starwards, petulantly stamping his heel, be-Jesus, casting down his bags – black plastic bin-liners I had insisted on, so much less suss than svelte pigskin valises.

Perhaps, I suggested acidly, he might consult the oracle? Often the best remedy in such situations.

Jaime tossed his coin, snatching only darkness on the way down, stumbling onto hands and knees, truffling knuckled tree roots, before he found it. That cast he declared to be 'foked up,' so he tossed again, and then again, since he didn't trust that decision. I knew the feeling well, but wasn't letting on, secretly amused by the sight of Jaime in a head scarf. Hermes, of course, raising between skirted knees, mascara staining sibylline cheeks.

'Come on,' I said, grasping his hand, 'We'll take the right

path.'

'But how you know it is not the other way, man?'

I smiled encouragingly, 'Whatever you like, sweetie. We'll take the left then.'

'But you just say is the other way? This is not like the city!' He stabbed a finger at three icy peaks above. 'These are the mountains of the foking *zipolotes gigantes*. You get lost up there, you foking die. Not even you foking bones to find.'

'Fok off!' That was me, dragging him to the right side, strength so much easier when responding to abject weakness. Giant birds indeed. Legends of the mountains, mere skeins of shifting cloud and shadow, baseless fabrications like that wooden imperial eagle on the wardrobe ... well, maybe not entirely baseless, sticky lies always carry a grain of truth, '*Like the condor, only they fly higher. So high you need a satellite to catch them.*' Yea, right, Joe! Nothing better to do all day in his cantina I suppose than tell tall tales. What had he called them? The *tzitzimime*. A ridiculous name. And then I remembered, the first morning, that huge raptor perched on a cactus. No doubt it was a trick of the light and the bird closer than it looked. Probably a large peregrine falcon, if they had them in Mexico.

Fifty yards up the steep path, I was brought up short by odd rumbles underfoot.

'Look!' That was Jaime, pointing back in the direction we'd just come.

Perplexed, I followed the line of his trembling finger, gasping as I made out a shaft of eldritch green light spilling the hollow of the ancient tree by the fork in the trail.

'Quick! This is not a good place,' Jaime said, hurriedly gathering his bags.

'But I need to see this!'

'You foking *loco*, man?' Jaime rasped, throwing off my hand. 'That is the death light of MictlAn-te-cuh-tli!'

'Mick who?' I dissembled, even as I realised the baleful light was my second intimation from the Lord of Death. The hollow trunk was the entrance of an ancient labyrinth that extended below the mountains, under the town and far beyond. There were lost cities down there, long since abandoned by troglodyte tribes, like the Hopi, who claimed to have ascended from a cavernous realm and had never lost the habit of living underground. If ever I had a chance for everlasting fame and fortune, this was it. All I had to do was enter by the trunk ... but I couldn't overcome my fear of what waited in that hidden realm, so I turned away, regretting my decision even as I ran after Jaime, scrambling up the path ahead.

17

THE ASCENT...

How long is an hour measured in footfalls? By the luminous dial of my watch, just that, but by any subjective measure, so much longer. Check the desert down there, all that sand, an eternity of pounding *sierra* rock, climbing this fucking mountain, and now that boxy barrier to surmount, grim adobe tacked to a black precipice, the shuttered village a haunt of '*ladrones*' – robbers and worse, according to Jaime. 'But there's no alternative. We have to go past the village,' I insisted, my voice sounding monstrously loud in the neck of the canyon where we were standing.

'Are you blind?' I rasped.'

'Yes, but do not you see?' Jaime said, hitting on Xochipilli and his nose bag - coke and plenty of it. 'There, by the big rocks, *ladronés* in the foking shadows.'

'Fok off!' Yea, that was me, playing the hard man when all I felt was fear. For all I knew, he might be right about bandits. Those gargoyle shadows, weird. But one of us had to play the role. 'Jaime,' I hissed, 'When you're paranoid, you see what you want to see.' I shook my head. 'How you survived so long in your line of work is beyond me, Mr *Narcotraficante*.'

'I foking survive because I always check the ground ahead.' Jaime lifted his skirt, revealing the antique pearl-handled silver pistol, tucked into black suspenders. 'Is lucky I bring this,' he grinned saucily, giving me the eye.

'Oh yea?' I nodded. 'One shot and you'll only wake the

whole village.'

Jaime brandished the pistol. 'And what is the alternative?' He scowled. 'I do not think you know anything, Mr Foking Expert.'

According to Gomez, the mountain Indians possessed a sixth sense, but they were also a superstitious lot, easily impressed by mendicant charlatans. Six senses be damned. We'd give them seven, with these plastic bags full of designer clothes, make like black, turbaned, giant ancestor spirits – how we'd scare the shit out of them. Did I really believe that? Not really, but neither did I believe Jaime and what he saw. Coke madness, that's all it was. Yea, I was infected too. I should never have taken that snort.

Walk tall, that was the way, the settling contents of drooping black plastic obscuring my vision, so much so I was unable to see the next step, let alone lurking danger. Lucky that, I was so intent, I didn't react when three gargoyles leapt out from behind the rocks and, screaming hairy curses, ran into the darkened village, disappearing down vertiginous alleyways. Incomprehensible curses now conjoined by cacophonous barking – wild echoes that persisted, long after we were through.

'Aaahooooo!' cried Jaime, winding up the opposition from a safe distance. '*Aaaaahhhooooooo!*' echoed a far crag – still wearing his turban, the mad Mullah of Mexico, doing his dervish dance, spinning closer and closer to the edge of the path.

'Aaaaahhhoooooo!' Nothing below, just total blackness and delayed action karma. Plenty of time to snort all that nose candy, numb to his brain when he finally hit base.

'*Oyé, hombre!*'

'*Qué?*' Startled, I looked up.

Out of the darkness, Jaime, advancing coyly, dangling a gold star from a striped ribbon. On tiptoes before me, like a pint-pot *presidente* awarding the *Croix de Guerra*.

'I take everything back, every bad thing I ever think or say to you,' he said, stepping back and saluting. 'From now you are *el generalísimo en la revoluçion*.'

'Really,' I gawped, baffled by his strange turn of behaviour.

'Yes,' he beamed. 'Think what we can do! No fok can stop such *fuerté*. not even the *pinché* NSA.'

I didn't know any ASN, possessing as I did a dyslexic's disregard for acronyms, but they sounded really bad. *Pinché* suits from *el norté*, I guessed, glad I was in Mexico, and not in *qué loco gringo*-la-la-land, even if only on an icy mountain path, ascending ever upwards. By my watch, over an hour since the mad Mullah routine, add that to the cracking pace, maintained all the way, and it translated as at least four thousand feet. A long way without any sign of the town.

Perhaps we'd taken the wrong turn at the hollow tree? With my track record, the path probably an old prospector trail, leading to cul-de-sac canyon and a used- up mine deep in the *cordilleras* – some *generalísimo*, me. Better not tell Jaime, he'd be too disillusioned. Best take a breather and cadge something to smoke. 'Hey, Jaime!' I called. 'I don't suppose you have any grass?'

'*Cómo no?*' Stopping, he rooted in a bin liner. 'What kind of weed you want, man?' he said, looking up.

'I have choice?' I said disbelievingly.

'You are talking to *el número uno narco traficante*,' Jaime grinned proudly, pulling out a crocodile-leather case.

'Give it here,' I said, snatching the case. 'I have to check the goods for myself.'

'That is my *generalísimo*.' Jaime gave me the standard fist and forearm *macho* salute. 'Such *fuerté*!'

Acapulco gold, Durango red, Mazatlan tops, Oaxaca black, Quintana Roo blue, all displayed in labelled pockets. The best Mexico could offer, and all mine, I considered greedily, amazed at such riches. So long since I had a smoke I couldn't remember, a poor state of affairs for someone who once prided himself on his connections. Still, I was back in the business. I was *el número uno narcotrafico's generalísimo*, I thought proudly, sticking skins together, my first choice Mazatlan tops, pungent bearded heads, crackling between my fingers, as I rolled a huge joint.

'Xochipilli!'

'What you say, Jaime?'

'The god says to say he like you.'

'That's good,' I blurted breathlessly, my neck follicles tingling with a rush of cannabinoids.

'He say you must look up,' Jaime said, in an awed tone. 'He send you a sign.'

'Whaa ...' I mumbled. What was he on about?

'Now!' Jaime repeated insistently.

For the first time that night, there was light on the mountain facing us, at our backs the new-risen moon, casting its mantle on the far crag like a diaphanous gown slipping old shoulders. Suddenly blazing from the summit, an awesome conflagration, the light of Xochipilli wafting silently upwards, for the briefest of moments illuminating the whole mountainside, before dissipating into space.[1]

Struck dumb, we both just sat there, staring out over the precipice. And then I heard it, a faraway mournful tolling of the bells of the cathedral. We were on the right path.

'... *diez, once, docé, trecé!*' I counted. 'That's lucky,' I said, springing to my feet at the thirteenth chime. 'C'mon Jaime! The town's that-a-way.'

---

1   An old tradition of prospectors in the *sierras*: concentrations of silver ore give off a gas that can be seen when the new moon shines at an oblique angle.

www.ingramcontent.com/pod-product-compliance
Lightning Source LLC
Chambersburg PA
CBHW030623130626
46552CB00002B/683